HOW TO CATCH A HAPPY EVER AFTER

SPECIAL EDITION

CHESTER FALLS
BOOK SEVEN

ANA ASHLEY

Illustrated by
COVERS BY JULES

How to Catch a Happy Ever After- Chester Falls Book 7
Original © 2021 by Ana Ashley
Special Paperback Edition: September 2023
ISBN-978-1-915031-11-2

How to Catch a Happy Ever After is a work of fiction. Names, characters, businesses, places events and incidents are either products of the author's imagination or used in a fictitious manner. Any resemblance to actual persons, living or dead, or actual events is purely coincidental.

Cover design: Covers by Jules

Editor: Abbie Nicole

Join Ana's Facebook Group Café RoMMance for exclusive content, and to learn more about her latest books at anawritesmm.com!

DEDICATION

To all the readers that have spent time in my Chester Falls
world, this book is for you.
Thank you for coming along with me on this wonderful
journey.

Ana

ABOUT HOW TO CATCH A HAPPY EVER AFTER

You are hereby invited to the wedding of the century.
Yes, you got it, Tom and Wren are getting married this Christmas.

Drama.
Sparkles.
Well intentioned, but meddling friends.
Surprise pregnancies...
...this wedding is set to have it all, including a brand new couple who is well overdue for their Happy Ever After.

They were the anti-heros. The bad guys.
When old wounds are healed, and new bonds forged, will Rory and Sergei find the courage to embrace their connection and find their own happy ever after?
This series finale is a tale of love, friendship, and the power of family and found family. Told from multiple points of view, How to Catch a Happy Ever After is not a standalone, but better enjoyed after previous books in the series.

RORY

It had certainly been more than a few years since I last stood in the center of the Chester Falls town square.

Despite the colder than usual fall, somehow everything was blooming. Proof, if any was needed, that the town had its own magic spell. Or maybe just a really good gardener.

The square, as well as the buildings surrounding it, hadn't changed much. I knew that because I remembered every single time I'd been here. And like most of the locations in the small town, the square held my secrets.

It was here that I had my first hotdog from a street vendor after the book fair when I was eight. My grandad had sworn me to secrecy because if my parents knew about it, they'd definitely forbid our weekly adventures into town.

That was the first secret I kept. Inconsequential, now that I thought about it, but it had a much longer-lasting effect on me.

Secrets existed.

Secrets meant I could do normal things.

Secrets kept me safe.

Until that safety became a gilded prison. A self-imposed retreat from myself. And who do you become when you can't be yourself?

In my case, an ugly, cold person who hurts others.

I shivered in the cold despite my heavy coat. Maybe I was just cold all over, and it had nothing to do with the temperature.

Taking a deep breath, I steeled myself for what I was here to do. I had no real excuse to turn back. Especially since this had been my idea. One that my therapist had encouraged.

I walked toward Fabulize, ignoring anything that might be a distraction, such as the man selling roasted chestnuts on the corner of the square or the street art exhibition from the high school art club students.

The door was closed, but the sign was turned to open. Not surprising, considering how cold it was outside. From the entrance, I could see the store's owner by the counter, drawing on a large notepad.

I pushed the door open, the bell giving away my presence.

"Good morning and welcome to Fabulize. I'm Tom, your new fairy godmother and granter of all your fashion wishes."

His smile warmed me up instantly. I'd heard some stories about Tom from my best friend, Connor, but my imagination didn't come anywhere close to what being in front of him was really like.

His eyes were a strange color that looked almost violet.

Were they real? Whatever they were, I couldn't take my eyes off him.

"Are you okay there, sweetie?" he asked.

"Yes...um, I'm sorry, you're just so much more than I thought." I blew out a long breath. "Sorry, that came out all wrong."

He smiled. "Oh, don't you worry. I've been extra since the day I was born. Besides, you can't wear this outfit without owning your sparkle," he said, running his hands down his waistcoat. It was purple with a gold embroidered pattern that looked like those fancy, old French chandeliers.

I nodded, unsure of what to say, and took the embossed wedding invite from the inner pocket of my coat, setting it down on the counter.

"I'm Rory."

I let my name hang like a curse. Well, it felt like a curse to me most of the time.

Tom stood up straight, and his smile went even wider. Then he came out from behind the counter and hugged me.

What's going on? I'm pretty sure this isn't how this is meant to go down.

"I'm so pleased to finally meet you," he said, releasing me. I missed his warmth immediately. "Connor talks about you all the time. I hope you're back to stay. I know he misses you, and James is one pet adoption away from owning a zoo to make up for it."

I laughed. I missed my best friend too. I guess I never considered that he might miss me too now that he was all loved up and married to his childhood best friend.

"Yes, I'm back. That's um...why I'm here," I said.

Tom nodded as he leaned against the counter.

"I don't know where to start," I continued, but Tom held up his hand.

"Hold on. Let me grab us some brownies and a cocktail."

"Cocktail?"

"Don't worry, it's non-alcoholic. I like to be sugared up for heart-to-hearts."

I did a double-take. "How do you know what I'm here for?"

He shrugged and disappeared behind a heavy curtain, coming back a minute later with a plate stacked with mini brownies and two tall glasses filled with a multicolored drink.

"Take a seat." He pointed to the couch.

I followed him and sat on the opposite side, wondering how this visit had turned completely upside down before I'd even said why I'd come to see him.

"Okay, my dear, tell me why you're here. And I hope it's not to decline the invitation to my wedding because it's no taksies-backsies."

He seemed so serious about it that I wasn't sure how to follow. Because he was wrong. I couldn't go to his wedding. I mean, after all I'd done, how could I?

"You're Charlie's best friend. I know he confided in you about us." I cradled the drink with both my hands to have something to do with them. "I'm really sorry about what happened. I've spoken to Charlie..." A lump formed in my throat as I remembered how easily he'd forgiven me when I really didn't deserve it.

Tom put his hand on mine. "You have nothing to apologize for. Not to me, at least."

"But I do. I know Charlie was alone with my secret until he confided in you. I know...you're still keeping his secret. My secret. I appreciate that more than you know, even if I don't deserve it. That's why I need to apologize to you. After I left Chester Falls, I tried coming back so many times, but each try failed because I didn't know how to handle things. I hadn't forgiven myself, and I wasn't ready to talk to other people. But I'm tired of hiding away. I want to live in the only place that ever felt like home to me. And I want to be able to wave to you on the street, to have you make me a suit for a work event, and to not feel like my past is constantly behind me, waiting to push me over."

Tom took a sip of his drink. "Rory, I only have one question for you."

I nodded.

"Are you still in love with Charlie?"

What?

"No. No. I mean, I love him, but I'm not *in love* with him. He's so happy with Kris, he's fulfilling his dreams, and he's a fucking prince now. A prince!"

Tom laughed. "Yeah, I'll never get used to that. I mean, if anyone was born to wear a tiara, it was me, right? It's a good thing Wren treats me like royalty," he said, shoving a brownie in his mouth in the most unroyal manner ever.

"Sorry," he said with his mouth full. "Can't get crumbs on this outfit, or it'll be a bitch to clean."

I held my drink to my lips. Tom was right, it was very sweet, but it was also the thing I didn't know I needed until I took a sip.

"Wow, this is ridiculously good, Tom. What's in it?"

"Wholesome rainbows and a little bit of fairy dust. It always works wonders on those who need a hug in a cup."

My throat tightened. If only Tom knew how much I needed a hug. Or human contact from someone that truly cared beyond the mutual agreement that our time together would be casual and secret.

Fucking secrets.

"Thank you, Tom. I wasn't sure how to do this, and I certainly don't deserve how easily you've forgiven me."

"Like I said, there's nothing to forgive. If you've made things right with Charlie, then you've made things right with me. Now, about the wedding..." he said.

"I can't go."

"Can't or won't?"

Neither, I thought. I could go to the wedding. It's not like I had a busy social agenda anymore. I also wanted to go, I just... "Maybe it's a bit too soon. It's one thing to make amends and another to join such an important celebration."

Tom grabbed the plate with the brownies and held it up to me. I couldn't resist taking one. He put the plate back on the small coffee table next to the couch and turned to face me. He suddenly looked serious, and I felt like this was a part of Tom he didn't often let out.

"My dads died when I was only a baby. Most of my life, it was just me and my mom, and then there was Charlie. I never thought my family would turn out to be made up of so many wonderful people. If I'd stayed in Boston instead of moving to Chester Falls, I would never have met Wren. Bottom line is, life is too short to live in the dark. Come to the wedding, have more drinks than you should, eat more than is wise, and be the Rory you want to be. Who knows, you may even find your own prince charming to kiss at midnight. It could be the start of your own happy ever after."

I laughed. "Okay, I'll come to the wedding, but as for the second thing...I doubt it."

"Why's that?"

I looked away. "That would mean I'd need to be out."

"Why aren't you? Sorry," Tom said. "No one should be out before they're ready, but wouldn't you be happier if you could openly be yourself?"

I shrugged. "I almost came out to Connor when we were fifteen, but I got too scared. My parents...they're not... I don't want to talk about them, but if I'd come out, I'd have lost the little freedom I had, including being able to see Connor. It was easier staying in the closet, and then it was just too late."

Tom stood up and went over to one of his display shelves, coming back a moment later holding a burnt-orange scarf in his hand.

He wrapped it around my neck and then placed a hand-held mirror in front of my face.

"Butterflies start out as larvae, the rainbow starts out as rain. You can come out in your own time, but don't walk out of this door thinking it's too late, Rory, because it's not. Whenever you want to do it, I can guarantee you'll be accepted. I don't know what your family situation is like, but here in Chester Falls, you already have one waiting for you."

I felt my eyes water and had to take a deep breath so I wouldn't cry. God, I was so tired of everything. All I wanted was to bathe in Tom's kind words and believe they were true.

"Thank you, Tom. You have no idea how much this means to me."

"I do, Rory. Trust me, I do. See? You already look like a different person. You can be what you want to be."

The way he said it made me wonder what he meant. It was hard to believe that Tom could be anything else but this kind, sparkly person in front of me. Then again, I knew how ugly the world was out there, so maybe he'd had his fair share of punches thrown his way.

I left the store with a promise to come back to get a suit for the wedding after Tom insisted I keep the scarf.

His words also stayed with me. Could I do it? Could I be an openly gay man?

Tom was right. I would be accepted. After all, Connor thought he was straight all his life until he reconnected with James, and out of all the challenges they'd faced, Connor coming out didn't seem to have been one of them.

The wedding was two months away, so I had time to think about it.

Not that I was hoping to find my happy ever after, as Tom had put it, at the wedding. That would be crazy.

Before I turned the corner to a side street, I saw Wren going into Fabulize holding a large coffee from Spilled Beans.

Wren was another guy from my childhood that hadn't exactly been straight and had come out after meeting Tom.

It seemed all around me were perfect examples of why it shouldn't be so hard for me to do this. Why did it still feel like I had such a big wall to climb?

WREN

One of my favorite things to do was watch Tom work when he didn't know he was being observed. He probably didn't even realize that he always had a permanent smile whenever he rearranged one of his displays or dressed a mannequin.

I usually did it when I stopped by Spilled Beans to buy him a coffee, indulging in watching the man that changed my life for the better before going inside.

Today was no different, except it took me longer to find him inside the store because he was sitting on the couch.

He never did that unless he was going through his designs with a customer, so I sped up my pace and forfeited watching him in favor of finding out what was wrong.

The bell on top of the door gave away my presence immediately. His smile when he saw it was me settled that pebble in the pit of my stomach.

"Hey, Angel," I said as he ran to me and jumped into my arms, wrapping his legs around my waist. Luckily, I was already used to Tom's special brand of greeting, so I managed to keep the coffee cup sealed without spilling a drop.

"You were out running when I woke up, so I didn't get my special morning time with your magic cock." His pout was so adorable I couldn't resist having a taste.

Tom's mouth was welcoming, greedy, and oh-so-kissable, as always. I swear that I could live more than three days without water if I had Tom's lips on me.

"I promise it won't happen again," I reassured him.

"Why did you leave so early? Don't you usually run with Aiden at lunch?"

"I still do, but I'm trying to fit in an extra run if I can. You won't stop baking, and I want to look nice for the wedding."

He did a double-take. "You don't want me to bake?"

"Hell no, baby. I don't want you to stop. But I want to walk down that aisle and have you look at me like you can't take another breath unless I'm yours. I don't want to give up your brownies, so I need to exercise."

I was also testing my own fitness, but I didn't want to tell Tom that. Since the last surgery, my knee had improved to a point where I didn't have pain after a longer run. I knew I was probably pushing a little too hard, but it was just something I needed to do.

Tom would worry too much, and he already had a lot on his mind with the wedding.

"Sprinkles, I already can't catch a breath when you're around, and you're all mine. Every single sexy, delectable inch of you is mine." He punctuated his words with small kisses that left me hard and needing more.

I walked farther inside the store, with Tom still wrapped around me like a cute monkey.

"Thank you for my coffee, Sprinkles," he said, taking the cup from me, which gave me the opportunity to put both hands on his ass.

As I carried Tom past the couch to the back office, I noticed a plate with some brownies and two cocktail glasses on the table.

"You had an early customer?" I asked.

Tom didn't answer immediately. I sat on the larger couch he had at the back, the one we'd had sex on multiple times, and took Tom down with me.

My dick was definitely enjoying the closeness, but I was more interested in knowing who Tom had seen first thing this morning.

"Rory was here," he said.

"Rory? Connor's best friend, Rory?"

That I was not expecting. I only knew Rory had been back to Chester Falls a couple of times in the last year because Connor had mentioned it when we all met up for drinks.

"I haven't seen him since high school. He used to be glued to Connor like peanut butter and jelly. What did he want?"

Tom took a long sip of his coffee and looked away from me.

"Angel...?"

He shrugged. "Nothing much. He got the invite to the wedding, and he might want a suit."

"He's coming to the wedding?"

Tom bit his lip and tried to take another sip of his

coffee, but I took the cup away from him. He huffed and crossed his arms over his chest.

I loved it when he was like this. Petulant with a dash of *how dare you question me*. It was adorable.

"Fine. I invited him because I figured it would be nice for Connor to have his friend back. I didn't know he'd moved back to Chester Falls, so I expected he wouldn't come. But I'm glad he is. I think it'll be good for him."

I narrowed my eyes and gave him his coffee back. Whatever Tom was up to, it couldn't be good, but I didn't have time to dig deeper because I had to get to work for the teachers' meeting before coaching.

"You have the kindest, purest heart of anyone I've ever met, so if you want to invite a man you don't know to the wedding to make his friend happy, then I'm more than happy to have him there."

Rory and I hadn't been that close at school. He was just one of the many kids in the same class and on the football team. If he was back for good, I'd need to tap him for my adult team.

"Thank you, Sprinkles." He placed the almost-empty cup on the coffee table by the couch and then resumed his place. This time draping over me like a blanket.

I wrapped my arms around him and relaxed under the soft kisses he placed on my neck. How I'd been so lucky to find someone like Tom to spend the rest of my life with, I didn't know, but I'd hold on to this feeling—to him—for as long as I lived.

"Don't start something you can't finish, Angel," I said as his hands roamed down and over my erection.

"Oh, I have no intention of finishing anything. I'm just warming you up for later. Pick me up?"

"Absolutely," I breathed out, trying to get my body into some modicum of decency. At least I already knew Tom's effect on my body, so I always wore my clothes to school and changed to my coach uniform there. Those loose pants were a lot less concealing of my erection.

I kissed Tom goodbye and left.

There was a crowd outside the school gate. I had my own parking spot, which was handy because there was no way I'd be able to park anywhere near the school today.

"Riley, over here!"

"Can we have an autograph?"

"Riley! Riley!"

I walked toward the gate and the group of people calling out someone's name like there was some kind of celebrity around. What the hell was going on?

As I approached, people made space for me to pass until someone grabbed my sleeve. "Mr. Mason, can you introduce us to Riley Dempsey?"

I laughed. "I would, but he'd need to show his ugly mug in Chester Falls," I joked, but as the crowd parted and I got a view of the school gate, I was suddenly faced with my old coach.

"I don't know, Mason. The missus thinks I'm quite the catch," he said, looking down at his still very much in shape, forty-six-year-old body. It was no wonder when the man trained with his team daily.

I smiled and walked toward him. "Coach Dempsey. What brings you to Chester Falls?"

I went for a handshake, but he pulled me into a hug. "If

I knew I'd have such a welcome reception, I'd have come sooner."

"Well, I'm happy to show you around. You scouting? I'm training the senior team in an hour," I said.

"I'm scouting, but not in the way you think."

What other kind of scouting is there?

He turned to the crowd. "Give me some time with my boy here, folks. I'll sign your stuff and take all the photos you want on my way out."

There was a loud cheer. "Thanks, Coach!" some guy said.

"Is there any place we can talk in private, Mason?" he asked.

"I have an office, but the moment we walk through the locker room, you'll be the center of attention again. Come this way."

I guided him through the football field to the other end, where we had a shed with sports equipment and some picnic tables. The kids liked to hang out there before practice, but they were all in class, so we wouldn't be interrupted for another half hour.

"So what's the deal, coach?"

"Mason...um, I guess you go by Wren these days, huh?" he asked, and I just nodded. "I have an offer you can't refuse."

He pulled out an envelope from the inside pocket of his coat and handed it to me.

"What's this?"

"I've spoken to the team doctor and the surgeon who worked on your knee. I'm happy to see you're fully recovered from your injury."

I ran my hands over my short hair.

"How do you know that?"

I'd seen the team doctor and the surgeon who worked on my knee after my injury, but I'd done it privately. They were the best, so when my knee started bothering me more than usual, I'd gone to San Diego to see them.

"Did they disclose my personal medical information?"

Coach raised his hands. "Not quite. You know the Marinos are a family. After you left, I realized I missed an opportunity."

"What do you mean?" The envelope felt heavy in my hand. Not because of its weight, but because I had a feeling whatever was inside was going to disrupt my perfectly crafted life in Chester Falls.

"I've been where you've been. An injury to my back ended my pro career, but I always knew coaching was my passion. I didn't want to come on too strong before you were ready."

"Ready for what?"

"To come home and work for me."

I laughed. "What? You want me to be an assistant coach for the San Diego Marinos? You're insane."

I turned around and walked toward the trees closer to the school fence.

"You have a real talent, Wren. You were a great player, and I keep hearing good stuff about your coaching skills. Didn't one of your students get picked up by a scout a few months ago?"

"Yes, he was already going to college on a sports scholarship. The scout only promised to keep an eye out for him."

He nodded. "You know as well as I do, that's part the kid's talent and part having the right coach."

"Coach, I have a life here. In case you don't already know, I live as an openly bisexual man, and I'm engaged to a man I'm marrying in just eight weeks. I can't upend my life and move to San Diego."

He put his hands in the pockets of his pants and rocked back and forth on his expensive shoes. "Son, sometimes in life, you get to a fork, and you have to decide which path to take. I have no issue with your sexuality, and neither will the team. Remember that hum you felt in your chest when you walked out onto the field and heard the crowd cheering? You can have that back. Plus a nice paycheck that'll set you and your future husband up nicely."

I shook my head. "I can't."

He walked over, took the envelope from my hand, and put it in my coat pocket.

"Just think about it." He tapped my coat and turned to leave.

I took a deep breath and ran my hands over my face.

No matter how good the offer was, there was no way I could move my life and Tom's to San Diego. What about Fabulize? I couldn't do that to him.

I would just ignore the envelope and pretend it didn't exist.

After all, I had a meeting and a training session. That was what mattered, right?

CHARLIE

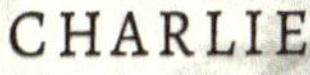

The ever-changing view of the palace gardens was mesmerizing as always. The trees were now a spectrum of color from burnt orange to deep brown. Soon many of them would be naked, ready for the winter snow.

When Kris promised I'd love Lydovia, he wasn't wrong. The four defined seasons were like catnip for an artist like me. I had countless drawings of the gardens on my sketchpad, and I was sure I'd keep adding more because I never got tired of the view.

I took a deep breath, wishing I could just merge with the landscape outside for a little bit. Feel the chilly wind on my skin, the crispy rustling of the leaves under my shoes.

Anything to take a break from my task list.

I closed my eyes as a finger traced the skin at the back of my neck. The little hairs stood to attention as a current of energy ran up my head, making me shiver.

"Hmm," I moaned, leaning my head forward to give him better access.

"What has you worried, baby?" Kris asked.

"You keep doing that, and I'll have no worries, ever. I'll just be nice and chilled...hmm..."

I groaned when he stopped, but before I even opened my eyes, my sketchpad was taken out of my hands and I was pulled onto Kris's lap.

"Hey," he said softly. His dark eyes never failed to make me catch my breath.

"Hey. God, you're gorgeous."

He laughed. "Thank you, baby. It bodes well for me that you think I look good."

"Psht, come on, you know how you look." I fisted his crisp white shirt and pulled him in for a kiss.

I melted under Kris's touch, like always. The way he kissed, his lips sucking mine into his warm mouth, his tongue opening me up, tasting me, and his hands. Fuck, his hands roaming my body. Even through layers of clothing, I loved the heat and sureness of his touch.

"Has your brain shut down yet?" he asked.

"Hmm? Who are you? Don't stop," I moaned, twisting in his embrace. Attempting but failing to straddle him.

"What are you doing?" he asked, holding me tighter.

"What do you think I'm doing?"

He took my hand, interlacing our fingers. Our wedding bands caught on each other.

God, we'd been married almost a year already, but it still felt like it was yesterday. Hell, some days I looked at him and the strength of my attraction and deep feelings for him still hit me like a truck with failing brakes.

"I think you're trying to avoid talking about what's on your mind," he said. "Don't get me wrong, baby. If I didn't think we could be interrupted, we'd be having this conversation naked. But since we're in the piano room, at best, I can play for you while you tell me why you're lost in your thoughts, gazing out at the garden."

I sighed. My erection subsided but didn't totally go soft. That was an impossibility as long as I was this close to my husband.

"The press officer keeps sending me emails about the new exhibition, the gallery has changed the opening night schedule three times, the students at the academy need help with their portfolio for the arts program, there are at least five dinners we can't miss in the next two weeks, and—" I stopped myself to take a breath because I could feel my anxiety spiraling.

I'd never been a particularly anxious person, but then again, I never in my wildest dreams thought I'd one day become a prince.

Me, Charlie Williams, the skinny redheaded boy from a small town in the middle of nowhere, who spent more time with his fingers dirty from graphite and his eyes on a sketchpad than playing outside with the other kids.

"Baby, you know we can cancel most of those things. Especially the dinners. We come first. Aleks will understand."

I smiled, my eyes moving to where his shirt opened to show his skin and a little bit of his chest hair. I dragged my nail over the little mother-of-pearl button at the top.

"Aleks is wonderful, but she needs our support, especially now." Kris's sister, the crowned queen of Lydovia, was pregnant.

The news hadn't been shared with the country yet but would be soon. I was surprised the press hadn't noticed how pale Aleks had been at her last address to Parliament. She wasn't having an easy time with her early pregnancy, and most days, she got sick more than once.

"She does, but she also has Phillip. He'll look after her, just like I want to look after you," Kris said. "Have you given any more thought to hiring a personal secretary?"

I shook my head. It was a ridiculous notion. I didn't have a particularly important job that required a secretary. I was more than capable of managing my calendar. It was just—

My phone rang on the side table, and Kris reached out for it.

"It's Tom." He handed me the phone, putting it on speaker.

"Hey, how's my favorite groomzilla?" I asked.

Tom huffed on the other side, which brought a smile to my face.

"I've not quite reached groomzilla stage, but if my to-do list doesn't ease up, I might end up conjuring the glitter zombie apocalypse by accident."

Kris snorted, and I gave him a pointed look.

"Oh, hi, Your Royal Sexiness. How are you doing today?" Tom asked in his typical glitter-wouldn't-stick voice, and I rolled my eyes.

"When will you stop flirting with my husband?" I asked.

"Um...never? He's on my list," Tom said.

"List?"

"Of the sexiest men I'll never bang, but if I get to, I'll let Wren watch. He has a list too, wanna—"

"No! No, thank you. You keep that to your weird selves.

Anyway, how's the wedding prep?" I asked.

"Couldn't be better. My event-planning skills run like a well-oiled machine...except yuck, I'm not getting anywhere near oil. It's gross. Anyway, I'm calling to ask when you're coming back. Will you make it to the bachelor party? Am I...getting a bachelor party?"

Ugh, I knew there was something else I was forgetting. Fuck. Fuck.

Kris must have sensed my distress because he answered for me.

"Don't you worry, Tom. Everything is in hand and on a need-to-know basis. At this point, you don't need to know."

"Ooh, intriguing. You got the cast of Magic Mike to strip for me, amiright? Oh, the glamour, the glitter, the abs..." Tom sighed on the other side of the line, and I knew he was distracted enough that I could avoid answering his question. "By the way, guess who came to see me?"

"Don't know, Jeffrey Dean Morgan?" I joked, knowing Tom's latest obsession with the actor.

"Uh, I wish...I'd lick those—um anyway, no, it was Rory. He's coming to the wedding."

Kris met my eyes, his eyebrows narrowing.

"That's great. Was he okay? We talked recently, but he didn't seem himself. It's like he's on a mission to redeem his sins, but the only person he needs to forgive is himself," I said.

"I told him as much. I'm glad he's coming to the wedding anyway. Connor will be there, and who knows, maybe he'll come out of his little shell and find some hot booty."

I laughed. That would be great, but I had my doubts that Rory was ready to come out.

Kris's lips turned up, and I gave him an inquisitive look, but he just shook his head.

"Righty-o, gotta go, boys. I have a makeover booked for a lovely sixty-year-old teacher who's going on her first date in years. I need to recharge my magic. Ciao!"

Tom ended the call, and I took a deep breath, pressing my forehead against Kris's chest.

"Baby, should we take a two-day trip to the cabin? I think you need some time away," he said, placing a kiss on my head. "I know just how to keep you distracted."

His deep voice so close to my ear made me shiver in anticipation, but...

"We can't, Kris. We have an adoption meeting with our attorney tomorrow."

My words hung in the air, heavy with meaning.

We looked into each other's eyes and smiled.

"Are you scared?" Kris asked.

"Terrified."

"What terrifies you the most, baby?"

I took a deep breath and looked away. "That I won't be a good dad. That I won't have as much time for Alexi as I want to, but most of all that he'll change his mind and won't want us to adopt him anymore."

"Hey, Charlie. Look at me, baby."

I met Kris's eyes again. All the doubts I had didn't seem to be reflected in his eyes. Was I making a big deal out of nothing?

"I'm being stupid, aren't I?"

"No, Charlie, you're not. You're going to be the most

amazing dad in the world. Let's face it, you already keep me on my toes. When was the last time you saw one of my lost socks under the bed?"

I hit his chest with my fist, but he caught it and brought my hand up to his mouth to kiss my palm.

"And we're busy because we do things that matter to us. All the charity work, the consultancy, the time spent working for other people. It matters because it changes lives. But we're first and foremost a family. It's because of the work you've done that we met Alexi. He will understand that," Kris said. "Don't get me wrong. He's a teenager, and as such, we can expect all kinds of wonderfully awkward things to happen at the palace when he moves in, but he loves you as much as I do. That I can tell by just looking at the two of you when you're in the same room. He looks up to you like you have the answers for everything."

"But I don't, Kris."

"Yeah, you do. And those you don't, we'll make up together."

Maybe he was right. We all wanted this. Alexi was ours. He'd been ours since the day I'd met him through our charity. His kind nature and talent shone through.

Kris had joked that he was a mini version of me, and if Alexi had red hair rather than blond, he'd think he was actually my kid.

I hadn't wanted something so much since I fell for Kris.

Now I just needed to figure out how to do everything I needed to do so I didn't miss my best friend's wedding.

Fuck, the bachelor party.

The ruckus outside my office was giving me a headache. I grabbed my least favorite stress ball and threw it in the direction of the far-too-happy guys in the main office.

"Keep it down. This isn't kindergarten," I shouted.

I could have the door closed, but I shared the office with Ryan Thomas, the head of security for the prince, and despite my seniority as his counterpart for the queen, I'd agreed with him early on that we operated with an open-door policy.

The guys out there weren't any less than us. We all put our lives on the line to protect the royal family on a daily basis. Ryan and I were simply the ones coordinating things.

"Hey, boss, want a doughnut? Luca got those apple ones you like," Zeke asked, rolling his chair to the aisle and throwing the ball back at me.

I caught it in one swift move.

"No thanks."

A moment later, Zeke stood in front of me holding a

paper plate with one of the pastries. I should have known he wouldn't leave it at that.

"I said I don't want any."

"Oh no, this one's mine," he said, stuffing half of it in his mouth. He smiled a powdered-sugar smile and swallowed it. "You've been so grumpy lately. Maybe you should get laid."

I sent him a look that would have sent other men running, but not much rattled Zeke. It was one of the reasons he was excellent at his job.

"I'm just saying, boss. All that pent-up...energy isn't good for you."

"What's not good for him?"

I groaned when I saw Kris walking through the door, clearly having heard Zeke.

"Sergei needs to get laid. Last week he sparred with Theo. Poor guy's DOMS had DOMS for days, and he's a boxing champion," Zeke said.

Kris raised his brows, staring at me. "Is that so?"

"Zeke, leave," I ordered. Thankfully Zeke knew exactly when I meant it.

Kris went around Ryan's desk and sat in his chair, swiveling it to face me and placing his feet on the desk.

"If you're looking for Ryan, he's not here," I said. "He took the afternoon off to go ring shopping. He's proposing to Luca at Christmas."

Kris snorted. "If you don't realize that I know where my head of security is at all times, then you don't know me very well."

He was right, but if he wasn't here for Ryan, what was he here for? Kris wasn't the usual stuffy prince. In his own words, he was just a public servant with good PR skills and a family name.

"Ryan is proposing?"

My head spun toward the door, where a wide-eyed Luca was staring at me.

Fuck. Can I catch a break today?

I let out a long sigh. "I'm so sorry, Luca. I didn't mean… fuck, I'm sorry."

He smiled wide. "It's okay. I'll handle it." He winked and then left to go back to his desk.

Kris had his hand over his mouth, clearly trying to contain his laugh. A pang of sadness hit. He never laughed so much when we were together. How long had he been unhappy with our relationship before he decided to break up with me? The thought was too hurtful to bear. Better focus on the here and now.

"How can I help you then?" I asked.

"I was coming to see if you'd like to train together, but now I'm more curious about what I just heard."

"You didn't hear anything but Zeke being his usual overbearing self."

He laughed. "Oh no, I got that. But why was he talking about your sex life? Or lack thereof?"

I leaned back on my chair. "Should I warn your husband about your sudden interest in my sex life?"

He snorted. "He's the one who sent me."

"Come again?"

"Charlie wants to know if you're going to Tom and Wren's wedding and if you're staying with us at our place in Chester Falls."

"No."

Kris threw me a challenging look.

"No to the wedding or no to staying with us? The place is big enough. I promise you won't hear our lovemaking."

I threw the stress ball at him, and he caught it, doing a little juggle with both hands.

"Both."

"You sure?" he asked.

"Pretty sure."

"Hmm, okay."

He took his phone from his pocket and flipped it around in his hands. "You want to give Charlie the news?"

I stood up to take the phone, but he gripped it close to his chest before I could get to it.

"Aww, big bad Sergei is afraid of sweet little Charlie," he teased.

I wasn't afraid of Charlie. I just couldn't deny him anything. The man was so kind and sweet that he hadn't just stolen Kris's heart, he'd stolen the heart of every single Lydovian, including my stone-cold one.

"Forgive me, but I'm not exactly in the mood to be around a bunch of loved-up couples for a whole weekend. I don't even know Tom and Wren that well."

Kris gave me another look. "You never seemed bothered before when we visited Chester Falls, and you already know all the guys well enough. Why now?"

The truth was too embarrassing to confess, even to someone who'd already seen me at my most vulnerable.

"Did you say you wanted to train? I have an hour before my next meeting," I said.

"Nice try, but you know I'm not falling for the change of topic. What's going on, Sergei?"

The worried tone in his voice made me cave. Because I'd never been able to deny Kris anything, even when we were kids.

"You know I've been lying low since the last scandal. I'm happy with my work here. I love the guys I work with. I just..." I sighed. "My social life has taken a dip, okay? I haven't so much as hooked up with anyone since—"

Kris leaned forward on Ryan's chair. "Since..."

I groaned. "Since the last time *we* were together." I closed my eyes, afraid to look at him.

The lack of any kind of acknowledgment about my confession caused a wave of anxiety to roll through me. I opened my eyes and stared at Kris. He wasn't exactly smiling, but I couldn't see any pity either. Thank god for small wins.

"You should go to the wedding," he said. "Treat it like a vacation. God knows you've earned it. Rory will be there, so you won't be the only single guy."

I laughed. "You're saying I should go because there is at least one unattached guy at the wedding," I deadpanned.

He shrugged.

"You know how ridiculous that sounds, right? I can't even begin to list all the things that are wrong with your statement," I said.

"Come on, I thought you two had a moment at Charlie's sister's wedding."

I let out a frustrated breath.

"That was two years ago," I said pointedly. "First of all, we didn't have a moment. Rory was somehow convinced that he could stop me from punching James, which I didn't do. Not because I couldn't have, but because I didn't want

Rory to get caught in the middle. Did you see the size of the guy? He's only a hair's breadth taller than Charlie."

"Uh-huh...go on..."

"Second, he didn't come across to me as being gay. Correct me if I'm wrong, but straight guys aren't usually into playing with other guys' dicks."

"Don't take your assessment at face value. Rory has many layers."

"I don't know what that means."

He laughed. "Come on, you always complained I was too big to be thrown around in bed. No danger of that with Rory. He might even be into it. Someone bigger, stronger, a little domineering..."

I shook my head. There was no way I'd be getting involved with what sounded like a serious closet case. No matter how good-looking I thought he was or how adorable I'd found his wanting to keep me separate from James. Or even how I'd noticed him avoiding me at Charlie's sister's wedding but caught him looking a couple of times.

No. I might not be able to avoid the wedding entirely, but I wasn't getting close to Rory.

No chance.

INDY

I always knew when I was alone in bed because Tate was so big and ran so warm that it was impossible to miss his absence.

His pillow had the mark of his head, but it was cold and the bathroom light was off.

There was only one place he could be.

I sat up and looked at my phone. Three a.m.

My alarm would go off in an hour anyway, so instead of going back to sleep, I went in search of my missing husband.

The dick fairy lights hanging from the frames in the hallway reminded me I needed to change the locks or take the spare key from my brother.

I'd hoped that by his mid-twenties, Sage would have grown out of the silly pranks and dick-themed gifts, but unfortunately, he was encouraged by our mother, who didn't have an appropriate bone in her body. At thirty, Sage, if anything, was getting worse.

He needed to find a guy who could keep his attention long enough that he'd forget about all of his prank plans.

I found Tate in the dark, staring at the crib in the nursery.

He was wearing his old sweatpants that hung so low on his perfect body that they never failed to make mine react. I knew from the front I'd be able to see where the *V* on his lower abs led to trimmed pubic hairs. With any luck, I'd see a hint of cock too.

He didn't move when I leaned against the nursery doorframe. A sign he was lost in his thoughts. I stepped forward until I was close enough to wrap my arms around his waist.

I kissed the skin between his shoulder blades. "What's up, baby?"

He turned around and held me tight, capturing my lips in a soft kiss.

"Nothing, just couldn't sleep."

"You also couldn't sleep last night and the night before. Either you've developed insomnia, or you're practicing for when the baby arrives. I'll make sure to remember that you're trained to be up all night."

He smiled against my lips. "You know I can be up all night." And then he nudged his hardening cock against my belly, causing my dick to stand at attention.

"I do know you can be up all night. More the reason to worry about your sudden nightly visits to the nursery. You do know there's no baby in the crib yet, right?"

He took a look behind his shoulder, but when his eyes met mine again, I saw all the pain and doubt he was trying to shield me from.

"You're worrying me, Tate. Are you having second thoughts?"

"No, Sweetbuns. I want nothing more than for our son to be here with us already."

"Then what is it?"

He ran his hands down my arms and took my hand, pulling me back toward our bedroom.

We settled in our usual position of Tate on his side facing me with his arm stretched out to serve as my pillow while I wrapped myself around him. Our faces were so close together that all I needed to do to kiss him was purse my lips.

I loved falling asleep like this. Often it started with soft post-orgasm kisses that slowed down as sleep took us until there was nothing but our lips blissfully pressed together.

"I guess I'm just scared that I'll be like my dad. Always working, never around. Hannah and I are so busy at the practice. What if I miss the baby's first steps? Or when he says Daddy for the first time?"

His words broke my heart. Tate was the kindest, most caring man. He'd literally take his shirt off to give it to someone else. Yes, maybe he hadn't always been like that, but his core was good.

"How long have you been feeling like this?" I asked.

"Since the day I saw a beautiful blue-haired guy walk into a bar. I was a goner the moment he slapped me. It scared the hell out of me that I already felt it even before I knew you were mine. But I know my past, where I come from..."

I reached out to touch his face and run my fingers

through his thick beard. He closed his eyes and seemed to relax under my touch.

"Tate, we all come from somewhere. What defines us is how we move forward. Before I met you, hell, even after I met you, I swore I wouldn't let myself fall in love with anyone because that would just lead to getting hurt. But I wouldn't change us for the world."

He smiled. "We never stood a chance, did we?"

"Nope."

"Indy, I need you to know that even though I'm shit-scared about being a dad, I'm also incredibly happy and lucky to be doing it with you."

"I know, baby." I leaned forward a little until our lips met. Our kiss was slow and unrushed like we had all the time in the world.

Our tongues barely touched, but the deep feelings transferred between us through our kiss made me feel safe, grounded, loved.

Some days I couldn't believe I would have this man for the rest of our lives.

"Tate?"

"Hmm," he hummed as he kissed my chin, my jaw, and started moving down my neck, giving me goosebumps.

"I don't have to get up for another thirty minutes."

"I know." His voice was thick with need, and just like that, everything shifted.

The sexual energy between us had always been strong and unavoidable. At first, it scared me because I didn't want to just be a hookup for Tate, not when I was so afraid of putting my heart on the line. But when we finally gave in...

"I need you inside me, Tate," I begged, pressing my

erection against his. He still had the sweatpants on, but they were baggy enough that with just one finger, I slid them down.

Tate raised his hips so I could push the sweatpants all the way off. The noise of his cock slapping his stomach made my mouth water and my hole clench. I suddenly had this raw need for Tate, and I didn't know where to start.

"Get on top of me, baby. Are you still lubed from last night?"

I chuckled. "You mean after you fucked me to sleep? I don't know, you tell me."

He reached behind me, and with little warning, put a finger in me. I rolled my eyes in pleasure, moaning when he pressed against my prostate.

"Jesus, Sweetbuns, you're so eager to have me again. It's like your hole is begging to be filled." He added another finger, swallowing my moans with his mouth as I started riding him.

"And this is news to you? I will always be ready for you."

I gasped when he replaced his fingers with his cock, but not from pain or discomfort. I always used to cringe when I read one of Aiden's books and the main character said his love interest's cock was made for him, but after Tate, I knew that was true.

Maybe I was just a greedy bottom with a size kink, but none of my partners before Tate ever felt this good. Then again, I truly believed Tate could be smaller or bigger, and it wouldn't matter. We would always fit perfectly together like apple and cinnamon, chocolate and caramel, peanut butter and jelly.

"Fuck, baby," Tate moaned when he bottomed out. He held on to my hips as I moved on top of him. Because I wanted to keep kissing him, my dick was hard and leaking, trapped between us.

I sped up my thrusts, trying to get more of Tate, more cock inside me, more friction on my cock. It was blissful and frustrating at the same time.

"Tate," I begged. I loved coming handsfree, but that usually only happened when we didn't have anal for a few days. Since Tate had tried to fuck me into oblivion last night...twice, I knew I'd need some help.

"Don't worry, baby. I'll give you what you need. Always."

With one arm around my waist and his free hand around my cock, Tate met his promise.

I freed my brain from any thoughts and let my body take over. We were a tangle of limbs, hands, lips. It was hot, sweaty, and so fucking good.

Tate grunted his orgasm, and the feeling of him filling me up with the way he held on to my cock triggered mine.

Afterward, we lay still, with me still on top of him. I looked at the clock and saw I had ten minutes before I needed to get down to the café.

"Now, this is the perfect way to start the day," I said. "Shower with me?"

"Absolutely."

"Let's do it. If you help me clean up, I'll buy you a coffee and breakfast."

He laughed and slapped my naked ass as I stood up.

With any luck, I'd get another orgasm in the shower.

Anything to take my mind off what I might find when I

went down to the café. I had a new assistant who was proving to be a little more than challenging.

I should have known better than to listen to my brother and accept his recommendation.

"You're thinking way too hard for someone who's just had sex," Tate said as we walked into the shower.

"Maybe you should do something about it," I said.

He winked.

I really did have the best husband in the world.

Whenever I had any doubts about my business decision to downsize and work with smaller businesses, all I had to think about was Olivia's lovely smile and her amazing cookies.

Cookies that very soon she'd be able to sell on her website, as well as cookie-baking kits.

"Thank you so much, Rory. I don't know what I'd do without your guidance. I don't even know why I was so afraid of doing this," she said, handing me a small bag with cookies. There hadn't been a single time I'd seen her that I didn't go home with a few cookies she refused to receive payment for.

"You make it easy for me, Liv. You just needed a plan to implement. You have a winning product already. The extra pounds around my waist are a testament to that."

"Bah, you're absolutely fine. Besides, I gotta keep you coming back for more, don't I?" She winked, and I smiled. Thankfully, Liv was on the friendly side of flirtatious. She was a genuinely nice person, and I was rooting for her and Lovely Buns, her bakery, success.

I left Stillwater and drove straight to Chester Falls.

Apparently, my presence was required at Spilled Beans. I should have known that accepting the invite to the wedding would get me roped into something by Tom.

I smiled to myself because as much as I could grumble about it, I was happy to be part of something good. I hadn't had that since I spent all my time with Connor in high school, and I was keeping such a big secret I don't think I ever allowed myself to really let go.

Tom's words had been on my mind since I last saw him, and I decided that I'd keep an open mind and see if I felt comfortable with the guys. Comfortable enough to come out.

Some days I felt like I needed to just blurt it out, and others, I just wanted to hide.

Determined not to let negative thoughts infiltrate my mind, I turned the radio on and listened to music all the way into town.

In contrast to the busy mornings, Spilled Beans was empty when I approached the door. Like in Tom's store, the coffee shop had a bell above the door. I thought it was quaint and adorable, like stepping into an old world.

"Hey, Rory. You're early, can I get you a coffee? Something to eat?" Indy said from behind the counter.

"Just a coffee, thanks. I was in Stillwater today and have some cookies for later," I said.

He pressed the button for the coffee in the machine and turned around. "Oh my god, do you mean Liv's cookies? They are the best. I mean, my cookies are great, but hers?"

He looked up toward the ceiling and closed his eyes, holding a hand to his chest. "Her cookies are divine."

I laughed. "I agree. Even if I feel a little guilty about eating them."

"Nonsense. Life's too short." He put the coffee cup on the counter. "Sugar and cream are over there." He pointed at a small unit by the wall.

I went over to add cream to my coffee and stopped myself when I saw the labels on the containers. Where the sugar label should be, it said *not salt,* and the stirring sticks said, *put this in*.

"Interesting labels," I said, trying to hold my laughter.

"Ugh, don't. My new assistant is convinced we need to juju up this place. Make it a fun place for people to hang out. And that,"—he pointed at the unit in front of me—"is his idea of fun."

"Has he not seen the lines outside this place every morning? I don't think you need to make it more fun. Your food is attractive enough," I said, stirring the coffee after adding the cream.

"Yeah, but the bags under your eyes aren't helping, honey. Here, I made some more labels." The guy couldn't be taller than five feet, wearing pink from head to toe and full makeup. His pearly-white smile was infectious, and I couldn't help smiling back when he turned to me.

"Hi, I'm Bubble, but everyone calls me...Bubble," he said, waving from behind the counter.

"Like bubblegum?"

"Like bubble butt." He turned around and did a little jig, not even the slightest phased by my comment, which I soon realized was a bit rude.

Indy must have seen my mortified look because he gave Bubble a pointed stare and took the labels from him.

"Hell no, I'm not calling the coffee machine a palate orgasm inducer," he said, placing the stash of labels in a drawer.

Bubble crossed his arms. "Why? You said more than once how my lattes are better than se—"

Indy put his hand over Bubble's mouth. "Don't you dare finish that sentence. The only reason you're still here is because your lattes really are...very good. But don't push it."

"Fine, don't take my awesome suggestions then. I'm headed home. You still want me in early on Saturday?"

"Yes, please, if you can. I have to make Tom's tasting cakes."

Bubble stared at Indy and put his hands on his hips.

Indy rolled his eyes and said, "Fine, your lattes are orgasmic. There I said it. Now go home before I put a label on your ass saying *fired*."

Bubble smiled all the way to the door, where he turned around and blew me a kiss.

"Nice to meet you, cutie pie."

I turned to Indy. "Where did you find him?"

"He just turned up one day like I repeated Beetlejuice three times."

I snorted.

"So, do you know why Tom called this meeting?" I asked.

"You can ask him yourself. He's coming over now."

I looked to the door and saw Tom crossing the road from the square. Ben was with him.

Tom was wearing a pair of really tight jeans and a

bright-yellow sweater with sparkly rainbows. Despite the cold outside, it looked like he hadn't bothered to put on a coat for the short walk from Fabulize.

His smile when he saw me was so infectious I couldn't help mirroring him.

He lived his life so authentically that I was always in awe of him.

Since meeting Tom, I'd been in his store a few times. He was making the suit I was wearing for his wedding, but with Connor living a few miles away in Windsor, Tom had become a friend, and I enjoyed stopping by the store to just talk sometimes. And I could be myself with Tom.

More than once, he'd asked me if I was avoiding Connor, and the truth was, yes, I was. I didn't want to lie to my best friend anymore, but I wasn't sure I was ready to come out, so I was in this limbo of avoidance.

"Okay, squad, are you ready for the wedding of the year? Hell, forget that. It's going to be the wedding of the millennium," Tom announced as soon as he stepped inside the coffee shop.

Ben smiled and shook his head behind Tom.

Indy disappeared into the back, returning a moment later with a couple of trays filled with finger sandwiches and cupcakes. Definitely more than four guys could eat. How many people was he expecting?

Ben and Tom put a few tables together, and Indy flipped the sign on the door to closed even though he left it unlocked.

It was clear that these guys were very close, and this wasn't their first rodeo. I felt like an outsider, unsure of my place in the group.

While the guys settled around the table, Tom came over to where I was standing a few feet away.

"I'm really glad you're here, Rory."

"Why exactly am I here?" I asked.

He seemed to think about it before he answered. "Charlie isn't here, which means I'm a best man down. The most important one, after Wren, of course."

I swallowed. "I'm...Charlie's stand-in?"

"Would you rather me tell you the truth?" he asked.

"Which is...?"

He put his hand on my shoulder. Even though Tom always looked like a dainty little thing, he was actually an inch taller than me, so I had to look up to meet his eyes.

"When I moved here, I didn't know anyone. I'd met Indy only a couple of times before and Charlie was in Lydovia. These guys welcomed me like I was the missing piece in their lives, but I think the puzzle isn't complete yet. There's a space for you."

I stared at him, my mouth open. "That's...that's the single most beautiful thing anyone's ever said to me."

"I know. I'm pretty amazing, right?"

The bell on the door dinged, interrupting us.

If I was already unsure of myself, staring at the four guys that had just come in made me feel even more like an inadequate ugly duckling.

Indy and Ben ran straight to the two guys, who looked like the mirror image of each other, except one of them was built like a truck.

"That's Tate and Tristan. They're Indy's and Ben's husbands," Tom said in a low voice. "The guy who's too gorgeous to be real is Aiden. He's a sweetheart, and the silver fox is his fiancé, Slade."

"Jesus, is everybody here a couple?" I asked before I covered my mouth with my hand.

"Yeah. Come on, let's join them. Wren is at practice, so you get to be my plus one."

Tom made the introductions while the guys attacked the food. Before long, all that was left were crumbs and empty coffee cups.

"Okay, Glammies," Tom announced as he stood up.

Everyone looked at each other until Slade said, "I knew this was a trap."

Aiden snorted, and Tate and Tristan looked at each other like they were communicating some kind of secret.

"Why are you calling us Glammies?" Ben asked.

Tom rolled his eyes. "It stands for GLAM, Glamorous Legion of Amazing Men, but it's a mouthful."

"That's what he said," Tate added, and everyone laughed.

"Okay, give it to us," Aiden said. "We can take it."

Tom held up a notebook and a pen. "Indy is making the cake, so he's off the hook."

"Yes!" Tate said.

"I said Indy, not Tate," Tom said, pointing at Tate, whose smile left him.

"Okay, just no glitter, okay? My life is already full of dicks," Tate said.

"Speaking of dicks," Indy said. "You know my brother owns the craft store in Stillwater? He's offered to supply anything you need for the wedding. Favors, decorations, table cards. You name it, he'll get it for you."

Ben raised his hand. "I thought last week he broke into your place and wallpapered your hallway with a dick pattern."

"You can only see the dicks if you get really up close and personal with my walls," Indy grumbled, and Tate gave him a look.

I sat back on my chair, wondering if I was having some kind of out-of-body experience because I understood the words being spoken, but I had no idea what they meant.

"I'd really appreciate that, Indy. Tell him I'll stop by the store next week to talk to him," Tom said.

"You're a brave man," Slade said.

"Didn't he decorate your front lawn with a giant dick statue as an engagement present?" Aiden asked.

"He did." Tom's expression became scarily evil. "And then I added a tub of glitter to his laundry detergent."

"Respect, man," Slade said. "Let me never cross you."

Everyone laughed, and I was inclined to agree with Slade.

"What else do you need?" I asked.

Tom looked at his notepad and sighed. "Connor and James have the venue, Ollie recommended a florist, and I'm working on the suits."

"How about the bachelor party?" Tristan asked.

"Got it," Aiden said, and Tom was visibly surprised. "I spoke to Kris this week, and we have a plan."

"A plan?" Tom asked.

"Don't worry your sparkly little self, Tom. We'll tell you and Wren where you need to be."

Tom sighed. "Okay." Then he tore a sheet from his notebook and passed it around. Everyone took turns putting their names next to the tasks Tom needed help with.

I really wanted to help, but I had no clue what I could contribute until I saw the list.

"I can do your table plan and some of these other things. I'm good with calligraphy," I said.

Everyone looked at me, and I felt my cheeks warming under their gaze.

"I learned it when I lived in Singapore," I explained, adding my name to the list.

Wren arrived shortly after, so between catching him up on the meeting and everyone chatting, we didn't leave Spilled Beans until it was dark outside.

I wasn't hungry for dinner after eating Indy's sandwiches, so when I got home, I went straight to the bathroom to grab a shower.

When I looked at my reflection in the mirror, I almost didn't recognize myself. I was...smiling.

I was going to help a friend. Maybe there was still hope for me. Maybe I wasn't as selfish and broken as I thought.

After my shower, I picked up my phone. Before I could talk myself out of it, I opened the messaging app and tapped on Connor's name.

Rory: Hey, can we meet up to talk this week?

TOM

"Okay, Coco, you be a good girl while Daddy and Papa are out, okay?"

Coco meowed her reply, which knowing her could be anything from "Please don't abandon me. How could you?" to "Who are you? I have important queen things to do. Leave now."

I held out my hand, and she bumped her head against it, requesting some petting, which I, as her human servant, was happy to provide. When she decided she was done with me, she hopped from the counter to the floor and sauntered to her castle in the living room.

"Babe," I called out to Wren. "Don't forget to drop Coco off at Gina's on Tuesday. She has a playdate with Cosmo, and I need to get to the store early to work on your wedding suit."

"Okay," he called back from the bedroom.

"Oh, and her favorite food is running out, so we need to remember to get some more."

"Noted."

I opened my wedding notebook on the kitchen table and looked at all the notes I marked for this week.

Usually, my color-coordinated scheme made it easy to not get overwhelmed, but with the number of things that needed to be done for the wedding, not even glittery ink worked.

I closed my eyes and took a deep breath through my nose. The scent of Wren's cologne, my favorite, filled my senses.

"What's the matter, Angel?" he asked, wrapping his strong arms around me.

"Just wedding stuff. It's a big list, and we only have five weeks."

"I thought you delegated some stuff to the guys," he said.

I turned around to face him. "I did, but there's stuff we can't pass on."

"Like cake tasting." He leaned over and pressed his lips against the side of my neck.

"Hmm, cake is good," I said, a shiver running down my spine, making my cock harden.

"I think you taste better." He sucked my lower lip inside his hot mouth, and then his tongue was seeking entry into mine. My brain shut down while my body took over, bending to Wren's demands, shouting *yes please* and *more* with a cherry on top.

"You can't feed me to the guests," I said as he ran his hands down my back, stopping when he reached my ass.

I put my arms around his shoulders, and he got the message. In one quick move, I was lifted onto the table.

"No, you're all mine, Angel."

God, I loved it when he got all possessive and demanding.

My notebook was forgotten, the list ceased to exist, and I became a soft piece of glittery playdough in Wren's hands. He put his hands on my chest, pushing me until I laid back on the table.

Today I was wearing a pair of black skinny jeans and a pink sweater that Wren had accidentally shrunk in the wash. Although considering the effect the short sweater had on Wren, I suspected he'd done it on purpose.

He ran his hands under the soft fabric and found my nipples, teasing them into a peak before focusing on my cock.

"I love it when you get so hard for me, Angel."

I bit my lip, tightening the grip of my legs on his waist. This wasn't going to cut it. I needed more friction, and I needed it naked.

"Wren," I begged.

"At the danger of sounding like a tease, we need to go, baby," he said.

"Ugh, you're evil. Why did you start this if you can't finish it?" I asked, sitting up on the table and letting my legs dangle.

And I pouted because anyone in my position would.

He cupped my face. "I did it because you needed to relax and forget about the wedding for a moment."

"Relax?" I asked in a high pitch, pointing at my dick. "Do I look like I'm relaxed?"

He laughed. "Poor baby. I promise I'll make it up to you later."

"You better," I muttered and got off the table. "Come

on, let's have cake. At least that always comes with a happy ending."

Despite the chilly weather, we decided to walk to Spilled Beans. Walking around Chester Falls was still one of my favorite things to do, even long after I moved here from Boston.

The Saturday market was winding down by the time we arrived at the square, so we went straight to the coffee shop.

"There are the happy grooms," Bubble squealed as soon as we were inside. "I hope you're ready for the tasting experience of your life. And no, I don't mean me."

We walked up to the counter, and he shimmied out to give me a hug. "Although I wouldn't mind your fiancé taking a bite," he whispered in my ear loud enough for Wren to hear. "I bet he bites good, amiright?"

I looked at Wren, who looked mortified, especially since there were two elderly ladies also staring at him from their tables.

"It's okay, baby. He's only an excitable mini-twink with far too much energy. He won't hurt you," I said, holding Wren's hand.

"The same could be said about you, and look where I'm at."

"Sparkles, you know I'm definitely not mini anything."

"Ugh, you better go out back before I have to call the paramedics for Winnie and Thelma over there," Bubble said.

Wren looked at the old ladies. "Those aren't their names, right?"

"They are now," Bubble said before he went back to his work behind the counter.

We found Indy in his kitchen virtually covered in flour or powdered sugar. It was hard to tell. He looked more than a little flustered.

"Oh, honey, that's wrong?"

He looked at us and then at the clock. "Fuck, is it three already? Fuck."

I went around the counter he had in the middle of the kitchen and put my hands on his shoulders. "Hey, it's okay. What do you need?"

He sighed. "I wanted to have a beautiful tray with your cakes all lined up, a few cocktails or coffee. This is a special day for you—"

"Indy, what happened?" Wren asked, standing next to me.

"Nothing's going right, and I think I may actually kill Bubble today."

"I'll help," Wren said, and I elbowed him.

"I'm starting to think he's immortal. I came down this morning to a hundred dick-shaped cupcakes. I had to make them into other...well, shapes," Indy said, looking really exhausted. "I squeezed his neck but had to stop when he asked me to tighten my grip. I swear to you..." He shook his head.

"What do you mean? He baked a hundred dick-shaped cupcakes? Why?" I asked.

"He wanted to help me because I've been a little stressed lately. Allegedly all he could find were these dick-shaped cupcake molds." He shrugged and then took a deep breath and shook himself off. "Okay, let's do this."

Bubble came into the kitchen with three coffees and

left. He looked as happy as anyone without a care in the world. Maybe he was a psychopath.

Indy left us to go get changed and came back five minutes later looking a lot more settled.

"You have six cakes to try. Three are the standard flavors: vanilla, lemon, and chocolate. I picked a different kind of icing for each, but you can change it if you like. The other three are a little different, but I think they could work really well."

Wren's phone dinged, interrupting Indy. He took it out, looked at the screen, and put it back in his pocket. "Sorry about that. Carry on."

"Everything okay?" I asked.

"Yeah, fine."

Indy placed the trays in front of us. "Okay, so the fourth one is a lavender-honey sponge with lavender buttercream. I really like this one. The honey is from Reed's farm, so you know it's local and good quality. The fifth one is a mocha-spiced cake. It's delicious and also fits the season. A Christmas wedding isn't complete without some kind of spice, right?"

"Gosh, I don't even know where to start. What's the sixth one?" Wren asked.

"That one is apple and caramel. Again, it's a good winter flavor, and I can add some spice to it if you like."

I tried the last cake first, and as soon as the taste of the caramel hit my tongue, I moaned like the sugar addict I was. "Holy mother of wedding cakes, this is amazing, Indy. What do you think, babe?"

Wren looked at me like he'd been lost in space. He

hadn't even tried the cake. "Oh, um, which one did you have?"

"That one," I said, pointing at the cake without taking my eyes off him.

"Wow, this is really good. Can we have this one?" Wren asked.

"You haven't even tried the others."

He winked at me. "Let me rectify that." He picked up a different fork and put it through the mocha cake.

I did the same. The cake was absolutely delicious, but I struggled to appreciate it because Wren was acting a little off.

"I like this one too, baby," he said.

As we worked through the flavors, Indy took notes. We couldn't decide on one, so Indy put another sample of each in a box for us to take home.

I was sure that's not how wedding cake tastings went for most people, but I guess being good friends with the baker helped.

It was starting to get dark by the time we left Spilled Beans. Bubble had closed up everything, and Indy promised me he'd go up to his place and spend the rest of the day chilling out with Tate.

Wren took my hand as we crossed the road to the square.

"What do you think the guys will do for our bachelor party? I mean, it'll have to be on different days, right? So they can attend both," he said. "Or will they combine it into one super-fabulous party?"

I stopped when we got to the square and pulled Wren's hand until we faced each other.

"I wonder if I kiss you now, which cake will you taste like," he said in a low voice.

I rested my head on his shoulder and took a deep breath, letting his cologne wash over me for comfort. Then I looked at his beautiful clear blue eyes, and all I saw was my Wren. The man I'd fallen in love with.

"Come on. I believe you made me a promise, and I'd like to collect," I said, lifting my heels off the ground to capture his lips.

"You want sex after eating six cakes?" he asked, wrapping his arms around me.

"With you, I'll always want sex. But this time, I want you to make it last. Make me beg for more. Fuck me into the mattress and make love to me like I'm unbreakable."

He closed his eyes, and I saw his Adam's apple bob up and down. I knew the effect of my words, but our winter coats served as a good concealer.

"Wren, nice to bump into you again."

We both turned to the man who'd called out to Wren.

"Coach..." Wren's voice broke a little. "What are you... erm, Coach, this is my fiancé, Tom. Baby, this is Coach Dempsey. He's the head coach for the Marinos."

I held out my hand. "Nice to meet you. Are you here to scout?"

"Something like that."

"We'll be landing in fifteen minutes, sir."

I looked up from my work at the ever-efficient flight attendant who worked in Kris's private jet.

"Thank you, Petra."

I closed my laptop and looked out the window at the moving landscape beneath us. Soon we'd be landing in the private airport near Stillwater, a few miles away from Chester Falls.

Every time I'd been to Chester Falls with Kris and Charlie, I'd enjoyed the family gatherings they attended. Charlie's mom's attempts at drawing me into the family were amusing, especially since I had to keep reminding her of my position as security for Kris and her son.

Caroline reminded me so much of my mom that I could rarely refuse her anything. Maybe the Williams family had some kind of special warm magic that drew people in.

Even my old friend, James, had ended up marrying Connor, Charlie's brother, who'd been his childhood best friend and first love.

When I'd pointed out to Kris that I'd be surrounded by happy couples, I wasn't exaggerating. Literally everyone in their circle was paired up.

Not that I was jealous, but my history as Kris's ex-boyfriend and my current position as head of security for the queen of Lydovia really made for a sad and lonely love life. Even hookups were out of the question.

The weather as we landed was sunny but chilly. The time difference between the two countries was significant enough that I knew I'd feel jet lag unless I had a good night's sleep.

"Petra, thank you for a good flight. Get some rest, and I'll let you know the next flight plans tomorrow."

"Yes, sir." She smiled and went back inside to join the crew.

The usual rental used to drive Kris and Charlie was replaced with something a little less stiff and formal and a lot more my style. Without them, I was just a civilian, and since they'd been kind enough to send me alone, I was going to enjoy every single mile of tarmac I burned with the Aston Martin.

After all, it wasn't often I enjoyed the finer things in life anymore.

The low traffic helped me get to Kris and Charlie's place on the outskirts of Chester Falls relatively quickly.

They'd wanted a house that was close enough that they could walk into town, and after many lengthy discussions, they'd agreed this place was perfectly secluded and safe. Mostly because the main entrance was off a side road, making it invisible to the curious minds that might be intrigued by the number of cameras by the gate.

At least the visible ones that had been placed to deter civilians. It was the carefully placed cameras around the property that provided the level of security I was comfortable with for Kris and Charlie.

Charlie had almost demanded that I use the trip to relax and treat it like a vacation, so even though I'd thrived on a routine when I'd been in the royal army, somehow, I forgot to check the security system before I approached the gate.

I pulled up my tablet and added the license plate for the rental car to the system, so it would be recognized by the surveillance system. A moment later, the gates opened, and I drove up the small road to the house.

Charlie had warned me Tom might drop by with some food on my arrival, so I wasn't shocked when I saw a car parked outside.

As soon as I got out of my car, Tom came running out of the house.

He stopped when he saw me next to the sports car, his face instantly taking a sad turn.

"Hi, Sergei. Um...did you have a good trip? You must be tired, right? I left you with some food in the fridge, so if you take a nap, you don't have to worry about finding something to eat."

"Hey, Tom," I said, bending my knees a little to meet his eyes. "They really hoped to make it, but a lot is going on out there."

Tom nodded, the corners of his mouth rising a little, but there was no happiness behind his eyes anymore.

"I understand. I mean, that's what you get for having a prince as your best man, right? At least I get bragging rights...if he comes to the wedding."

The last part was spoken so quietly I almost missed it.

"Hey, Charlie wouldn't miss your wedding for the world, okay?"

He nodded. "I know. I just...I'd swap whatever big surprise he's organized for our bachelor party in exchange for having him back here just for the weekend."

I didn't know what to say. This was exactly why Charlie had pulled all the strings he could to give Tom and Wren a really great time.

"Trust me, he wishes he was here. After all, it's not every day that—" I let my words hang as Tom opened his eyes wide and showed me his first real smile.

"He won't break, baby," Wren said, coming out of the house to join us.

I laughed. "What can I say? I was trained by the best. As adorable as you are, I'm afraid my cold black heart won't take pity on you."

"Ugh, when will we know? I mean, how is a girl meant to prepare? Do I need accessories? Are we dressing up? Are we traveling?" he asked.

I shook my head. "Nope, we're staying indoors, listening to Alanis Morrisette, and painting each other's toenails."

Wren laughed. "You know that's a perfect night in Tom's world. However, I hope Charlie and Aiden remember there are two guys in this wedding. As much as I'm happy to have my toenails done, I'll be disappointed if there are no strippers."

"You'll have to wait and see. It all shall be revealed tomorrow." I went around the car and took my suitcase from the trunk.

Tom and Wren followed me inside.

"I've started a fire for you," Wren said. "I know this house is all futuristic, but there's nothing like a cozy fire in this weather."

"I made you some cupcakes too. They're in the kitchen. Will you tell us if you need anything?" Tom asked.

I smiled. "I'll be fine, thank you. I appreciate your welcome gesture. I'll admit it's a little strange being here without Kris and Charlie."

"You know we'd have you at our place, but the spare room is currently the wedding HQ," Wren said.

"I'll be all right here. It's not for long anyway."

"Oh really...?" Tom said, coming closer and batting his eyelashes at me.

I laughed at his attempt to get more information out of me and took some pity on him. "I'll let you know tomorrow evening."

"Speaking of which, the guys are coming over to our place at six tomorrow evening for some drinks. We hope you can make it," Tom said.

"Six? I thought they were coming at seven. It's Ro—" Tom ran over to Wren and put his hand over Wren's mouth. "You have such a bad memory, babe. We changed the time because...um...I don't want to go to bed late. You know I'm following a strict pre-wedding beauty regime."

I didn't dare ask what that was about, so I thanked them again for their warm welcome and walked them out.

With the doors locked and all alarms outside engaged, I moved to the living room where Wren had started the fire. Despite the size of the house—after all, it could house all of

Charlie's and Kris's families plus staff—it still had a homey feeling.

Charlie had taken inspiration from his own home growing up and filled the walls with photos. The carpet was deep and soft, and there was a balanced amount of modern furniture. He'd hired his friend's husband, Tristan, to work on the redecoration, and it had paid off.

If I was ever in a position to own a similar place, I could see myself sinking my feet into a deep-pile carpet while cozying up to my husband under a soft blanket on the couch.

I must have fallen asleep on the couch because when I opened my eyes, it was dark outside. The fire was running low, so I added a couple of logs and went to the kitchen in search of some food.

My phone dinged with a message just as I plated my lasagna.

Charlie: Hope you arrived safely. Enjoy the vacation. That's an order.

Kris: You heard my husband.

Sergei: I'm trying to decide which room to defile first. Yours looks rather comfortable.

Kris: I swear to god, Sergei...

Sergei: You shouldn't have let me come unsupervised. You know what happened last time.

It was a low blow, but he knew I didn't mean it. Hell, the last few months, Charlie had been so adamant about me dating again that I wouldn't be surprised if he wished I would bring someone over.

A cold shiver ran down my spine when I remembered the stories Charlie told about his Aunt Gina.

Anytime I saw her, I found her too scary. I wasn't sure if it was the long, red nails, the big hair, or the fact that she was definitely much smarter than she played out to be. But anytime she visited the palace or this place, I always made an excuse about checking the perimeter of the house.

I sent one last text to Charlie, begging him not to send his aunt to check on me. I'd do anything he asked without question if he saved me from her claws.

I was coming out of the shower when my phone dinged again.

Charlie: Ask Rory to be your wedding date, and I'll make sure you're safe from Gina.

RORY

om lived in the same neighborhood Connor had grown up in, so it was easy to find his place. It didn't surprise me that they'd picked the area to live in. From my memory, it was close to Wren's parents and ideal to raise a family.

When I was a kid, I'd always preferred these houses to the large mansion I lived in. There was no warmth, no personality, and it certainly never felt like home, unlike Connor's parents' place.

Once I found a parking spot on the road, I took my supplies from the trunk and went up to the house.

"Hey, Rory, come on in," Wren said, opening the door wide so I could get through with the large box. "Tom is with Sage in the spare room with the craft supplies...or whatever they're meant to be."

I chuckled as I followed Wren to the living room. "I take it this kind of stuff isn't really your jam."

He pointed to the coffee table, so I put the box down.

"I always think that my life is distinctively split BT and

AT—Before Tom and After Tom. You remember how it was. There was nothing else but football in my life. The times my dad had to pick me up from school because I lost track of time training." He shook his head. "But then Tom came along and changed everything."

"Was it hard?" I asked.

"I never imagined I'd learn how to bake, let alone win a bake-off. And if you ever told me I'd end up with a shelf full of sparkly products in my bathroom, I'd have laughed. But...Tom is the sunshine that lights up my life. Without him, everything would always be the same. Boring and colorless. So, no, it wasn't hard. How about you? Did you leave a broken heart behind in Singapore?"

I smiled and shook my head. "Nah. No one for me. I have another box in the car, so I'll get that one."

As I turned to the hallway, Tom came out from one of the rooms. I didn't recognize the guy behind him laughing until...I did.

"Rory, you're here," Tom said cheerfully. "This is Sage, Indy's brother. Although you probably know each other, right? I keep forgetting everyone went to school together."

Sage held out his hand for me, and I took it, avoiding eye contact.

"I went to a different school," Sage said. "Nice to meet you. Are you from around here?" he asked.

"Um...yeah...kinda. I need to get a box from my car. I'll be right back," I said, turning around and heading for the door.

"I'll walk out with you," Sage said. "Tom, let me know if you need anything else. See you soon."

Sage didn't say anything until we were out of earshot.

"So...Rory...nice name."

I opened the trunk of my car and then turned to Sage. "Um...thanks for not outing me."

He stared at me with his deep-green eyes. "It seems that was a happy coincidence. I was simply trying to avoid personal questions, and from the look on your face when you saw me, I assumed you didn't want Tom to know that we know each other."

I ran my hands through my hair.

"We don't know each other, not really," I said.

"You're right. I didn't know your name, and I didn't know you knew my brother or his friends." He leaned against the car and crossed his arms over his chest. "But I do know you. I know how you flush easily when you're turned on. I know how you're afraid of asking for what you want, but your body tells no lies. I know—"

"Please stop." I held my hand up.

"What's up? Was my assessment incorrect? I mean, it was a while ago." His smile reminded me of the reason I hadn't been able to resist him.

It was one of my rare trips home from Singapore. My parents had demanded I attend a function with them, so I'd come home.

Well, not really, because I hadn't seen Connor, and being in Chester Falls was just painful. But Stillwater was close enough. Sage had caught me in a weak moment when I'd been reconsidering my life choices and hoping to find answers at the bottom of a beer bottle.

I let out a breath. "Sage, I'm...I'm not out with my friends, okay? I know it sounds stupid, and even more so at my age, but I'm not out, and I need some time to work it out. Please don't tell anyone."

"Hey," he said, his voice taking a surprisingly gentle tone. "We've all been there. Well, maybe not Indy and me. I swear my mom asked for two gay sons because she knew way before we did. Anyway, it's a personal thing. Once you come out, you have to do it time and time again. You'll never stop coming out, so when you do, make it count. Make sure it's what you really want and that you're ready. All I can promise is that it gets better."

"So I hear. I think…I want to be ready. I'm not scared of coming out. I just feel really stupid for not doing it already. Anyway, thank you, I appreciate you being supportive. I guess it shouldn't surprise me you're an actual nice guy, after what you did…" I let my words hang because I didn't know what I was going to say, and I was feeling too hot all of a sudden.

Sage came closer and put his hand on my shoulder. "Just so you know, I don't usually spend the night. I just felt like you needed it that time. The guys are superstars. You'll have nothing but support from them. Hell, with the stunts I've pulled, I'm surprised any of them are still talking to me."

Now that I knew who was behind the infamous dick gifts Indy complained about, I couldn't help smiling.

"It's nice meeting you, Sage," I said.

"Likewise," he replied, taking my hand and squeezing it a little.

Sage went over to his car, and I took the additional box inside.

Tom was on Wren's lap in the living room, and they

seemed to be just talking while petting the cat asleep on Tom's lap.

It took a while for my presence to be noticed, so I just stared at them like a voyeur. It was wrong, but I couldn't look away.

The cat raised its head and jumped up from Tom's lap to another couch.

"Um...do you want me to show you what I have?"

"Yes, yes, yes! I still can't believe you can do calligraphy. Will you teach me?" Tom asked.

I smiled. "Of course. It's not that difficult. It just requires practice. The benefit is that you get an excuse to shop for stationery."

Tom stood up like he was on springs. "Now you're talking my language, sweetie. Let's go."

I followed Tom to the spare room.

"Whoa, did a glitter bomb pregnant with rainbows explode in here?"

"This is my sanctuary. Where I create some of my best work. When I'm here, I feel like anything is possible. It reminds me to stay authentic, and it makes me so darn happy. The wedding stuff is actually in those boxes," he said.

I unpacked my boxes onto the large table. "I can do a few different fonts, so I'll show you a sample of each so you can pick."

"Oh dear god, these colors are beautiful."

"I know. I'm a little bit of a pen whore. I have all kinds. Even if I don't use them for anything, I just love writing with them." I picked a pen that had a long brush tip and a card. I wrote *Tom and Wren* in metallic gold before tracing over it with a different pen that left behind a rainbow hue just on the edge of each letter.

"This is beautiful, Rory."

"Thank you."

I never got praise from my parents, and since my grandparents died when I was still quite young, I rarely got it from other sources. Playing football at school was probably the only time I'd been praised for doing a good job, so I didn't quite know how to accept it from Tom.

"I need to show this to Wren."

The doorbell rang as he walked out of the room.

"Rory, honey, do you mind getting that?" Tom shouted from the living room.

"Sure."

Tom had told me the guys were coming over for a few drinks, but I thought we'd have a bit longer. The wedding was four weeks away, and I wanted to make sure I could make everything in time.

I put my pen down and went over to the door.

My chin fell when instead of Indy, Tate, Ben, Aiden, or any of the guys, I found myself face to face with Kris and Charlie's bodyguard, Sergei.

The first time we met was a clusterfuck.

The second time could go down in history as a reel of what not to say in the presence of the sexiest man alive, especially when you're a sad closet case.

"Rory, what a pleasure. May I come in?"

"Thank you...I mean, yes..." I left the door open for him and went straight to the spare room to hide. Maybe once all the guys were here, no one would notice if I sneaked out.

SERGEI

J couldn't say I was entirely surprised when Rory
mumbled some words and then ran off. After
all, it wasn't the first time he'd done it.

It still piqued my curiosity. Did he do it to everybody?
Or was it just me?

I'd been about to get out of the car when I saw Rory
and another guy come out of Tom and Wren's place, and
even though Rory walked in front of the guy, he hadn't
exactly been running away.

I'd recognized Rory immediately. Even almost two years
later, the man was still as beautiful as ever. With his dark
eyes, dark hair, and small frame, he couldn't be more opposite from me.

Maybe that was why I'd been instantly attracted to him
when James and I had been ready to go at each other's
throats. His reaction didn't match what I'd seen from him
after.

Rory had gone straight to the car parked in front of
mine. I'd stayed still, wondering if at any point either of the

"

two men would see me, but it was dark enough outside that they'd missed my presence.

I couldn't hear what they'd been saying, but their body language made it clear they knew each other. Still, something had been off.

The other guy looked like he was happy to see Rory. His relaxed smile as he leaned against the car and tilted his head toward Rory showed familiarity. I didn't like it.

Rory, on the other hand, had looked like he'd rather be eating glass. His expression changed as the conversation progressed, but he still looked uncomfortable.

My training taught me to see cues in people's behavior, and Rory was one of those complex characters that drove you to figure out what was inside. What made him tick.

There was also a vulnerability in the way he mostly avoided eye contact. As though he was afraid that if someone really looked at him, they'd find something he wasn't ready to show.

After the other guy left, Rory stood in place for a moment before picking up a box and going back inside the house.

I couldn't make myself leave the car immediately. I didn't want Rory to think I may have witnessed his conversation with the other guy, but I also wanted to make sure *I* was ready to see him.

Kris had told me Rory had been invited to the wedding, but I'd been too busy preparing my team for my absence to consider what being around Rory would be like.

I'd met most of the guys Charlie had grown up with. They were great people, and I was glad Charlie had them because it meant he retained a sense of normalcy in his life.

And I was also happy for Kris because all he'd wanted growing up was to be a regular person. Something he could be around these guys.

The problem with the over-familiarity and no-filter of these guys was that they'd sniff out any attraction I had toward Rory. If he was, as I suspected, still not out to his friends, then I didn't want to put a spotlight on him.

I was still standing by the door when Tom came into the foyer.

"Oh, what are you doing by the door, you big, hunky piece of broody sex-on-legs," Tom said. "Come on in."

"You know, men have died for calling me less than that."

He waved me off. "Meh, you wouldn't kill me. I'm too adorable."

I suppressed my laughter and followed him into the room Rory had run to earlier.

Rory was hunched over the table, writing some stuff on cards. There were several different fonts and colors.

When he spoke, he only looked at Tom, and even then, he wasn't really meeting his eyes.

"This is the extent of my skills. Any of these fonts will read well on larger cards as your table placements," he said.

Tom gasped like a kid who'd just walked into a candy store for the first time. "I might need some time to pick the right one."

Rory smiled. "You just need to pick the font. I can use any color or mix them up if you like."

I watched them as they became engrossed in their task. Tom asked Rory to try different color combinations once he decided on a font.

Rory seemed completely at ease around Tom and even cracked a few jokes I wouldn't have expected from him. The thought that Tom knew him better than anyone else, including me, made me jealous, which was utterly ridiculous.

Why would I even care?

"Okay, Glammies, I'm going to help Wren with the food. If you could bring those boxes out to the sitting room and unpack, that would be magnificent."

Tom disappeared again, leaving me alone with Rory, who started packing up his pens into a wooden box but left the cards out on the table.

He didn't look at me until he noticed I hadn't moved an inch and he needed to pass me to get to the boxes.

"What did he call us?" I asked.

"Glammies. It stands for Glamorous Legion of Amazing Men. We're his...squad."

I laughed. "Are you serious?"

The look he gave me said he was.

"What are you doing here?" he asked, almost aggressively. The kitten-with-sharp-claws type of aggressive.

"Shouldn't I be here?" I asked.

He stared at me, a little frown appearing on his forehead.

"I mean, can I get past?"

I leaned back on the chair and crossed my arms.

"Which question would you like me to answer first? Why am I here, or if you can get past?"

"I don't care, just let me through, please," he said.

"Hmm, I think you missed me. I didn't think I made that much of an impression last time, Kitten."

"We barely talked, and it's been two years. *And* don't call me that."

I extended my hand to him. "Okay, let's start over. I'm Sergei."

He stared at my hand and then my face. I could see he was torn between being civil and being clear about keeping his distance.

In the end, just like a kitten needing a belly rub, Rory gave me his hand.

His skin was warm and smooth, but there was no softness in his shake. He was making a point.

I turned his hand and brought it up to my lips, kissing it gently. "Nice to meet you, Rory."

When my eyes met his, I changed my mind. He wasn't a kitten. He was a little prickly hedgehog, and he was ready to strike.

I released his hand and picked up all the boxes Tom needed in one go.

"Beast," he said in such a low voice I wouldn't have heard it if there was anyone else around.

I turned to face him, keeping the boxes steady. "You have no idea."

He gave me a murderous look that turned into a predatory smile as he walked around me.

"If you came to help, you should have worn something less...expensive."

I was going to ask what he meant when the doorbell rang.

Tom rushed to get it, and all the guys flooded the foyer.

"Sergei, dude," Tate said, taking a couple of boxes from

me and creating an opening between the guys so we could walk through to the sitting room.

"Did I hear Sergei?"

"No," I answered before James had me in a headlock.

The remaining boxes were taken from my hands by someone, and I used my new advantage to tackle James until I was straddling him on the carpet.

"Now this is what I'm talking about," Indy said.

"Shirts off," Ben added.

"I should have charged an admission fee," Wren grumbled.

"Waaaait! Stop it." Tom shouted, and everyone went quiet. "I don't have the appropriate kind of snack for this show, so please head over to the table, pick up a plate, a drink, and a pair of gloves."

"I'm sorry, what?" I said. "What do we need gloves for?"

Rory snorted as Tom replied, "The glitter, of course."

I looked around, and there wasn't a single guy that looked like they thought what Tom had said was strange. They just made an orderly line for the table.

"Um, Sergei?" James called, reminding me I still had him pinned to the ground. "Okay, you win. Can I get food now?"

I stood up, and Connor came over to give me a hug. "Nice to see you, Sergei. How are Charlie and Kris?"

"They're really good and sorry they can't be here."

He smiled, but his disappointment was visible. I really hoped Charlie and Kris would come clean before their friends suspected something was up.

James gave me a friendly pat on the back and put his

arm around Connor. Together they picked up a single plate to share.

I wasn't particularly hungry, so I grabbed a drink and sat on a chair by the couch where Tom, Indy, and Ben were sitting. I saw Rory had chosen a chair farther away from the group.

Not far enough that anyone would notice, but enough to not be part of the group that surrounded the boxes on the coffee table.

Our eyes met for a moment, and despite our earlier friction, Rory looked at me as if he knew I understood him.

As the only two single guys in the group, we should band together against the couples. I just needed to convince him first.

My phone buzzed in my pocket, so I took it out and cleared my throat. Aiden looked at me and nodded.

"Attention, everyone. First of all, I'd like to thank you for having me here among your group. It's really an honor, and trust me, I don't say that lightly. After all, some of you have met the gang I usually supervise. Charlie and Aiden have been working hard to bring Tom and Wren a really special bachelor party, especially since Charlie can't be here."

Everybody perked up at the news about the bachelor party. Tom had his hand over his chest and was holding on to Indy.

Aiden continued, "So without further ado, you are hereby instructed to pack your suitcases for warm weather because this weekend..." He paused with everyone hanging on every single word out of his mouth. "We're going to Vegas, baby!"

Everyone cheered and started talking loudly to each other. Once again, Rory stood in his corner, staring at his drink. I got up and sat next to him.

"What's up, Kitten? You don't like Vegas? You know, what happens in Vegas stays in Vegas."

He looked at me, his eyes wide and his mouth slightly parted.

I couldn't take my eyes off his as Aiden announced, "One rule. No one can get married."

I'd visited Aiden's parents in New York before and had experienced the kind of luxurious life that came with having more money than you could spend in a lifetime. The personal chef, the maids, the driver.

It was surreal, and I was always glad to go back home with Aiden, especially since the work on our house had been finished and we could move in.

The house turned out to be absolutely perfect for us. It was big enough that we weren't on top of each other, but it was also cozy. I transformed the garage into my own play area where I restored old bikes, and the work on Aiden's writing office by the stream had just been completed.

Our first Christmas at the house was going to be perfect. Just Aiden, me, and Harley. We didn't need anything else.

However, I wasn't going to deny that traveling to Vegas on a private jet was an experience I'd never forget.

I hadn't had much time to prepare for the trip, but I still managed to buy new clothes and pay the barber a visit.

Most of the time, I smelled of oil and wore stained clothes. It came with the job, and I knew Aiden didn't mind. In fact, he seemed to have a kink for it, often coming to the shop after I closed and joining me in the shower.

But this time, I wanted to be a proper gentleman. Wear nice clothes, smell nice, and look like I belonged with Aiden by my side. I was damn fit for my age, but I was still the oldest guy in the group by far, and while I knew it didn't bother Aiden, I just wanted to look good for him.

"All right, guys," he said, holding up a bunch of envelopes. We'd been waiting in the lounge while Aiden checked us all in with Sergei's help. "Here are your room keys. Slade, me, Tom, and Wren are staying in a suite on the top floor. We have two bedrooms and a sizable lounge, bar, and separate kitchen and dining area. The suite will be our HQ. The rest of you will have your own rooms. You can thank Charlie for that."

"So, what's the plan after we drop our stuff in the room?" Indy asked. Tate whispered something in Indy's ear, which made him blush. I didn't need to guess what it was because as soon as my man had fulfilled his best-man duty, I was going to take him up to our suite and make him forget about everything for at least a couple of hours.

"We're meeting back here at midday for a dance class," Aiden said.

Tom squealed, Indy and Ben stared at each other, and the other guys looked like they were already planning their escape.

Aiden continued, "After the class, you have some time to chill. Hit the pool or the casino if that's your thing. I'll repeat again...Do. Not. Get. Married while in Vegas."

"Jeez, a guy does it once..." Indy mumbled, and Tate laughed.

"Best night of my life," he said.

"You don't even remember it," Indy said, and Tate shrugged.

"How about tonight?" Tom asked.

Aiden looked at me, and I gave him a reassuring smile.

"Tonight, we'll be split into two teams: Team Sprinkles and Team Beefcake. You can guess which one belongs to which groom. Me, Indy, Connor, Rory, and Ben will start off the night with Tom. Slade, Tate, James, Sergei, and Tristan will start off with Wren. There are two events planned. At midnight we'll swap, so each of us gets to party with both grooms-to-be."

"Um, Aiden, is there a reason all the couples are on separate teams?" Tristan asked.

"Yes, so you don't run off with your husband before the end of the party and go off adopting a camel or something," Aiden said.

I snorted behind him. "Baby, why would we adopt a camel?"

"I don't know. People do crazy shit when they're in Vegas, and let's face it, half of this group is already married, so what else can they do?"

I laughed and then overheard Ben whisper to Tristan, "Can we really adopt a camel?"

"Anything you like, baby," he replied.

"Okay, people. You know what to do. See you at midday." Aiden turned to me, looking buzzed and tired at the same time.

"Come on, baby, let's go chill in the bedroom," I said,

holding his hand and pulling the suitcase behind us.

"What if I don't want to chill?" he asked.

I pulled him closer and wrapped my arm around his waist. "I'm counting on it."

Even though I'd witnessed all the calls Aiden had with Charlie to plan the trip and had even seen photos of the rooms, it still hit me that we were experiencing the kind of extreme luxury I hadn't even conceived of while growing up.

Aiden closed the door behind us and started checking the room.

We had a perfect view of the strip and the fountains. The room didn't have a balcony but the wall-to-wall glass panels made for an astonishing sight.

Aiden came from behind me and wrapped his arms around my waist.

"What's up? Are you tired?" he asked.

"No."

"Then why are you so quiet all of a sudden?"

"Do you ever wish you could live like this?" I asked.

"Like what?"

"Expensive hotel rooms. Trips to luxurious destinations. People working for you."

"No. I have no desire to have any of those things. Maybe I'm privileged enough to be able to turn my back on that life, but the life we have is perfect. Just us and Harley, our new home. It's all perfect. I love going grocery shopping with you. Arguing over which brand of laundry detergent is better, adding extra items and then forgetting something else really important."

I turned around. He kept his arms around my waist

while I cradled his cheek. "You're forgetting fighting with Harley for her to stay home while we go out shopping and trying to convince her we're not leaving forever."

He smiled. "I love you so much, Slade. I'm so lucky to have found you, and I wouldn't change that for anything in the world. Now, what's it gonna be? Are you going to fuck me until I'm dead, or what?"

I tilted my head and went for his neck, sucking a patch of skin I knew would leave a mark.

"You don't need to stake your claim, baby," he said. "I'm wearing your ring already. Besides, do you think anyone would dare get close to us?"

"They better not even think it."

I pulled him over to the bed, removing his shirt and then mine. He undid his pants, and in a second, he was naked, his cock hard and ready.

"I can fuck you into oblivion, baby. But is that what you really want?"

He bit his lip and nodded, scooting up onto the middle of the bed.

I stepped out of my jeans and underwear and went to our suitcase to retrieve the lube. By the time I went back to Aiden, he was running his finger over his hole with one hand while the other stroked his cock.

"Starting without me?"

"Warming up for you."

"I thought that was my job." I put the lube aside and pushed his hands away. Aiden cursed when I ran my tongue over his hole, licking it like the best dessert. I loved rimming him, feeling him relax under my touch until he begged for more.

"Slade." His hoarse voice made me so fucking hard. I loved that he was so desperate for more that he met my tongue with his own thrusts.

"Turn around, baby," I demanded. "Hands behind your back. Yes, like that. Fuck, you look so beautiful. So mine."

"Always, Slade. But please give me your cock, or I'll change my mind."

I straddled his legs and grabbed the lube, applying a generous amount to my cock because I knew Aiden would beg for me to not prep him. I still added some to his hole, but he groaned when I tried to add a finger.

With my dick seeking entrance, I held his hands and pushed my way in slowly.

"Fuck, Aiden. I'll never get tired of how tight and hot you are."

"Argh...fuck...more, Slade, please..."

I pulled back until I was almost all the way out and then pushed back in, craving Aiden as if I wasn't already so connected to him.

He was flat out on the bed, so I knew I couldn't go as deep as I wanted to.

"That's it, Slade. Fuck me until all I can feel is your dick. God, I'm so fucking hard for you it hurts," he cried.

"I love it when you talk dirty to me. Aiden Lawton, always so proper, well-spoken, so perfect, coming undone for me."

He tried to raise his hips, but I was too heavy for him. Instead, I tightened the hold on his hands and fucked him harder and faster.

His moans were muffled on the bed cover. I covered his

body with mine, keeping hold of his wrists, and turned his head to the side.

"Are you ready to come for me, baby?" I whispered in his ear.

"So fucking ready."

My orgasm was right under the surface. My body was shaking with anticipation. But my man needed to come first.

"Do you need to touch yourself?" I asked.

"No...just, oh fuck, like that...keep going."

I rested my head between his shoulder blades while the lower part of my body did all the work, thrusting into Aiden with a desperation I felt in my core.

"Aiden," I shouted as I fucked my orgasm into him when I wasn't able to hold off any longer.

He groaned as he came. His pale skin flushing a beautiful pink.

I didn't want to leave his body just yet, so I released his hands and moved us sideways so I could spoon him from behind.

"I fucking love you so much, Slade. You always know what I need," he said.

"It's my job, sweetheart. I'll give you what you need for as long as I'm physically able to."

We stayed in the same position until my dick was soft enough to slip out of him. We took a slow shower together, and I set an alarm on my phone before we went back to bed for a nap.

From what I'd heard, the guy giving us the dance classes was ex-military and took his job very seriously.

RORY

 tried to hide in my room, but I should have known it wouldn't work. At five minutes to midday, just as I was ready to play dead, the door to my room opened and a far too cheery Tom walked in.

"Dude, what are you doing? What if I was naked?"

"Please, Sergei's downstairs, so I knew you'd be dressed." He went straight to the wardrobe and started pulling out my clothes. "Right...leave it with Uncle Tom, and you'll come out of this room looking like—"

"Hold up," I said. "What does Sergei have to do with this, and why are you making a mess in my room?"

Tom held up a shirt and a pair of slacks. "I'll pretend I didn't hear that last comment. I'm here simply to perform my magic. As for Sergei...I don't know. I thought I saw you two exchange a few looks at my place."

I huffed. "That was me threatening him with a painful death."

"Hmm..." He held up another shirt, throwing the other one on the bed. "And the look he gave you?"

"I don't know. I avoided looking at his stupid perfect face and crystalline blue eyes."

"Hmm."

"What's with all the hmms?"

"I'm diagnosing you with a big case of the denials."

"Thank you, Doctor Jones. I didn't realize I signed up for a session."

Tom let out an *ah-ha* and came over to where I was standing by the window.

"Put this on."

I rolled my eyes but did as I was told. I was starting to think nothing would get in the way of a Tom makeover.

"Are you going to stand there and stare?" I asked.

"Yes."

"Jesus Christ. I'm starting to think I should have just accepted going to hell and never asking for forgiveness." I took off my shirt and put the other on before doing the same with the slacks.

"Wow, *that's* what you're working with? My friend, I'm going to introduce you to the benefits and pleasure of fitted shirts," Tom said.

"This *is* a fitted shirt."

He snorted.

"What?"

"Rory, my sweet, beautiful new friend. You have washboard abs that go on for days. It's a crime to keep them hidden under a loose shirt."

I shook my head and put my shoes back on.

"Am I okay?" I asked, doing a full turn for him.

"I'll need to check your evening outfit, but for now, that'll do."

He came closer and started straightening the collar of the shirt. "Did you mean what you said?"

"When?"

"About regretting asking for forgiveness?"

I smiled and took his hands in mine. "No, not really. You've been a great friend to me, and even though I feel totally out of place with the guys, I am glad that you're making me part of your wedding. I feel very privileged."

Tom hugged me tightly. "Come on, let's go downstairs before the drill sergeant comes up for us."

"Sergei?"

Tom stared at me for a moment and just smiled. "No, I meant the dance instructor. I hear he's quite tough, but I like that that's where your mind went." He patted my arm and walked toward the door.

Minutes later, we were all walking inside a large studio with mirrors all around.

A loud whistle sound played. We all went quiet until a tall man wearing head-to-toe army gear came over.

He circled around the group with his hands behind his back as if he was rounding us up.

"Good afternoon, troops. I am Sergeant Quickstep, and I'm here to make sure you're all prepared for the event that will shape the rest of your lives. As I always say, if you want to be shaped by the event, you need to be in shape for the event."

I heard a snort and looked at Indy, who disguised it with a cough.

"This session is going to test your fitness limits and your mind. You will leave here today a new person."

"Sergeant, um...sir," Ben said with a lot more bravery than I had. "How long is this session going to last?"

"It'll last as long as it needs to last." Everyone shook as the man shouted his words, which in the big and mostly empty room, sounded even louder.

"Let's get started with a warm-up."

The sergeant put us in a line and asked us to run in place for five minutes and then do a hundred sit-ups.

"Is this really necessary?" Tristan whispered.

"Fuck knows," I whispered back.

"A hundred pushups. Now!" the guy shouted.

I had no clue what this had to do with dancing, but there was no way I'd speak up.

All around, the guys were working up a sweat and starting to get out of breath, especially after the sergeant demanded a hundred jumping jacks. What was his kink with the number one hundred?

"Wait," Tom said, leaning on Wren, who looked as fresh as if he'd just showered. "Hold on, sir. I have to catch my breath."

"How often do you exercise, son?"

"Every day. I'm a runner. I run from my problems, I run late, and I run my mouth," Tom said.

Indy snorted, followed by Connor, and before I knew it, everyone had broken down. From the corner of my eye, I saw Sergei. He was looking at Tate and laughing too. A beautiful, perfect smile that made him look young, carefree, approachable.

I looked away before I was caught.

The whistle sound played again. Everyone went quiet,

but as the sergeant was about to speak, the studio door opened and a woman wearing a hotel uniform barged in.

"Sergeant, I have a room full of bleach-blonde hair and fake tits moaning that their boot camp session is late, and they had breakfast this morning, so they're going to be fat for the wedding."

The guy stared at us and then back at the woman. "This isn't the wedding boot camp room?"

"For fuck's sake, Earl. This is Vegas. There are at least twenty wedding parties per hotel on the strip."

She looked exhausted and frustrated.

"Sorry, Mel," the guy said. "Let me catch up with the girls. I'll make it worth their while."

"You better," she said.

He turned to us and saluted. "At ease, soldiers. You did well. Please don't give me a bad rating. My boyfriend wants another dog, and this gig is all I have."

"You're good," Wren said.

"Gentlemen," the woman said. "Please accept my apologies for this mistake. Our dancing tutor caught the flu and couldn't come in today. Earl sadly has a habit of not reading the signs on the doors. I'm afraid we can't offer the dance class you booked, so I'll give you a full refund and send a special package to your suite in time for your party tonight."

I looked around and never saw so many relieved faces.

"Thank the lord of glitter bombs because this is more moving than my poor body is used to. I might need to apologize to my balls for making them sweat so unexpectedly," Tom said.

"TMI, dude," Tate said.

"I speaketh the truth," Tom replied.

"Well, if no one has any objections, I'm going to grab my husband and hit the pool. I like the idea of staring at his ass in tight shorts for the foreseeable future," Tristan said.

Tate bumped his brother's fist.

Everyone muttered their agreement and went their separate ways. I'd already spent time in the room when we arrived, so I walked in the direction of the hotel foyer.

"Hey, Rory."

When I heard my name called, I took a deep breath before turning around.

"What can I do for you, Sergei?"

"You can let me keep you company."

He put his hands in his pockets and leaned back on his heels, looking relaxed and self-assured. I didn't know why, but it annoyed me.

"No." I turned around and went for the door. I made it all the way outside until he caught up with me.

I tried to ignore him, but he didn't leave, so I stopped. "Don't you have something better to do?"

He shrugged. "Actually, no. It's a beautiful day, and it's not too hot. I thought I'd walk around the city, see the sights. Looks like you're doing the same."

"I'm not."

He tilted his head. "You're...not? You're outside, on the sidewalk, and up until a few seconds ago, you were walking."

"Ugh, why can't you leave me alone?"

"Is that really what you want?" he asked.

I huffed. "Yes! I don't know. I'm sorry."

"Look, I think maybe we started off on the wrong foot.

Even though I'm mostly a miserable grump, the guys have taken me in. I'm starting to think they have a savior complex or something."

I smiled. Sometimes I felt exactly the same way.

"Why don't we get to know each other a little better, and then you can decide if you still want to kill me or not."

I shook my head. "I don't want to kill you. I just don't get you. Then again, I don't get myself either, so it's not personal. It seems I'm not picky."

"Come on," he said, nudging his head. "Let's go explore Las Vegas."

I sighed. "Okay, fine. Lead the way."

SERGEI

Having Rory agree to my company for the afternoon felt like the biggest victory yet. This was my opportunity to spend some time with him and figure out who he was.

I didn't even understand why I had this compulsion to do it. Okay, so he was a sexy prickly little kitten, but so what? I'd met plenty of similar guys before.

"So, where do you want to go?" he asked.

"The fountains?"

"Is that a question?"

"Will the answer be yes?"

He gave me a challenging smile. "What if the answer is no?"

"How many questions do you think we can get through to decide whether we're going to the fountains before we get to the fountains?" I asked.

"Hopefully no more. Look." He pointed to the other side of the street, and sure enough, I could see part of the fountains.

I grabbed his hand and ran to the zebra crossing that had just turned green.

We got to the fountain just as a song was ending and another one started. The fountain came to life again with the accompaniment of "Time to Say Goodbye" by Andrea Bocelli.

"I looked this up before we traveled. They play songs that are synchronized with the water spray," I said, unable to take my eyes off the amazing show.

Rory didn't say anything, so I looked at him. I was surprised to see his eyes on me.

"What?"

"Nothing," he said, moving his head toward the fountain.

"It's not nothing."

He smiled. "It was a little adorable how you got excited about the fountain and the music."

"But isn't it great? I mean, the skill it takes to coordinate something like this must be phenomenal."

"Yes, I guess you're right," he said.

We watched the show until it all stopped after a couple of songs and then resumed our walk.

"Can I ask you a question?"

Rory looked at me, and I could see he was debating his answer.

"It depends on what the question is."

"What if I ask the question first, and then you decide if you want to answer it or not?"

"But then, if I don't want to answer, I'll still be thinking about the question, why you wanted to ask it, and what's going through your mind that made you want to ask the question."

My laughter came out unexpectedly. I was starting to really enjoy this back and forth with Rory. It was challenging and interesting.

"You'll never know unless I ask the question, will you? And what if I don't ask the question, and you always wonder what was it I wanted to ask?"

"Fair point. Ask your question."

"Why do you always set yourself just a little apart from your friends?"

Rory frowned. "Has anyone mentioned anything to you? Fuck, I don't want them to think I don't enjoy their company or anything. They're great. If anything, I don't—"

"Hey, breathe," I said, placing my hands on his shoulders. "No one has noticed. I did because...it's a habit to notice things and people."

"Okay."

We resumed the walk, but Rory was so quiet I wasn't sure what was going through his mind. Maybe I put my foot in my mouth by asking the question.

"Do you want to grab something to eat? I'm also a little thirsty," I said.

He nodded, so I pointed to a coffee shop with outdoor seating just opposite a chapel.

We ordered a sandwich and a cold drink and sat outside.

"I don't do it on purpose," he said, breaking the silence. "When I left, there was no one. I mean, Connor was at home, but that was it. When I came back, suddenly everyone was part of a group. They all became close friends, and I couldn't figure out where my place was. I was always *Connor's best friend* like it was a title." He shrugged.

"I get it. It's hard to fit in when you don't think you can or that you're not good enough. Trust me. I know that very well. But the guys welcomed you. It sounds like they genuinely care about you."

Rory seemed to think about it. We finished our sandwiches and drinks. There was no rush to go anywhere, so we stayed there, watching people.

Well, Rory might have been watching people. I was watching Rory.

After a while, the bells in the chapel rang, and after a moment, a couple came out accompanied by Elvis and Marilyn Monroe. They had confetti thrown at them and then took some photos in front of the chapel.

"They look so happy," Rory said. "Do you think they eloped? Or they always wanted to marry here?"

I looked at the couple again. The woman had short blonde hair and was wearing a short white dress. The guy wore a white suit and black shoes.

"I don't know. They look happy like they really love each other. Whether they eloped to escape or planned it, what matters is that now they have what they want."

"What's that?" he asked.

"Each other," I replied.

Rory finished his water and then put the glass back down on the table.

"I did something terrible. I hurt someone who didn't deserve to be hurt. That's why I don't feel like I have the right to fit into the group. I've asked for forgiveness, but I don't know how to forgive myself."

He was playing with the label on the bottle of water, so I reached out and took his hand.

"We may have more in common than we think, Rory. Maybe that's why there's this weird energy between us. Do you feel it?" I asked.

He nodded.

"For a long time, I thought I would need to play the outcast. The sinner who did everything wrong. The immature guy who was stupid enough to get caught with bad people. It was all lies, but the consequences were unimaginable. Do you know about me and Kris?"

"A little. I've never read gossip. I just know you used to date."

I nodded. "We've been best friends since before we could walk. We were our first everything, so it was only natural that our relationship progressed into something more. But we were never meant to be. We were just too scared about the possibility that we'd need to find someone else in a world we didn't know much about. I'm not royalty, but I grew up in the palace."

"That sounds quite sad. Not being exposed to things other kids take for granted, like playing football in the park."

I smiled. Rory hadn't taken his hand away from mine, so I kept rubbing circles on his palm.

"It wasn't too bad. We also had things other kids didn't. But the point is that when Kris and I broke up, we were just two guys who loved each other but weren't *in love* anymore. Kris reached that level before I did, and then I was caught in a spiral out of my control. I'm not going to make excuses. Some of it was my fault because I knew exactly how the press was going to behave."

"When I met you, all of that had just happened," he said.

"Yes. And Charlie, who quite rightly stole Kris's heart, was so perfect for him that he managed to save not just Kris but me too. It didn't take long until I was forgotten, which allowed me to focus on my work more and fade into the background."

"How did you come out of the shadows?" he asked.

"It wasn't overnight. Sometimes I feel like I was pushed into the light by Charlie's stubbornness and kindness. My friendship with Kris is stronger now, and I'd take a bullet for Charlie, not because it's my job, but because he's a better person and deserves to be alive."

Rory stared at our joined hands like he was in a daze. "He is. Charlie is so good and pure."

I thought I saw Rory's eyes water a little as he mentioned Charlie, but he looked away and then stood up.

"Let's keep walking."

I got into step with him. "So, what are you going to do?"

"About what?"

"Forgiving yourself?"

He shrugged.

"Rory, no one is perfect. We've all made mistakes. Did things we wish we hadn't. But life threw you a raft, and you're still holding on to the edge as if you're waiting for someone to throw you off."

"You're very insightful for someone who's mostly grumpy and serious," he said.

"Like I said, I'm used to watching people."

"And what do you see when you see me?"

I stopped and turned him to face me. In the distance, the fountains had started their show again.

"I see someone who wants to belong. Someone who wants to help others. Someone who is still finding himself. Someone who has a good core but is a little prickly around the edges."

He smiled, and for the first time, I saw his walls come down. He didn't say anything else, but I could feel it. Suddenly Rory wasn't just the good-looking man I'd met two years ago that still filled my thoughts occasionally.

He was now the person I knew. He'd let me in. Now all I needed to do was not screw it up. With my track record, that wasn't an easy thing to do.

TOM

"Jesus fucking Christ, Angel," Wren gasped from the door to the bathroom.

I smiled and turned around slowly. "You like?"

It had taken me a few evenings, but I'd hand sewn a rainbow of sequins to my skinny jeans that started at the seam of one leg and worked its way up to the waist. I paired it with a T-shirt and a waistcoat that continued the rainbow from the front to the back.

The best feature was that the sequins would glow in the dark, so once we were at the party, I'd be a dancing, glittery, glow-in-the-dark rainbow.

He walked up to me slowly, and I could see it in his eyes. The raw desire, the love, the need to rip my carefully picked outfit into shreds.

"Wait up, you can look, but you can't touch," I said. "This is an expertly crafted ensemble that needs to stay in place at least until midnight. Then and only then can you peel it off me."

He let out a sound that was something between a groan and a growl. "This is my bachelor party too, you know? Why do I have to wait for my fun?"

I put my hands on his hard chest. It never failed to get a shiver out of me whenever I touched him. "Think of it as delayed gratification...or edging."

He laughed. "Baby, neither of us is very good at edging."

"You can still kiss me though. If you think you can do it without messing up my outfit," I said.

I felt my body light up as he leaned down, placing his hands on either side of me on the sink. He ran his nose up my neck, inhaling deep. I shivered.

"Hmm, Angel, you smell delicious." He peppered my skin with light kisses that were starting a dangerous fire. If he kept going, I would call off the party and stay in the room.

"Where are the grooms?" Ben shouted from the suite living room, followed by a knock on the door.

"If you're naked, I swear to god..." Indy threatened.

"Saved by the crazy party boys," Wren whispered.

I stared into his eyes, reaching up to touch his face. "I love you so much, Wren. I can't wait to be married to you."

"Me too, Angel. Me too."

"I hear honeymoons don't require the presence of other people. Of course, that would depend on where we're going."

He laughed. "Nice try, baby."

I followed him out of the bathroom, appreciating the perfect fit of his gray slacks. I'd really enjoy peeling him out of them later.

The guys cheered as we came out into the living room. Wren took my hand and twirled me around. "Isn't my future husband stunning? You guys better take good care of him out there because he's just too delectable right now."

"One more touch," Aiden said. He went to his room and brought out a bag of tiaras. "This is for safety, so if we lose anyone, we can just look for the tiaras."

"You might be underestimating the number of tiaras present in Vegas," Tristan said.

Aiden shrugged, "Whatever, we'll just look great anyway."

Once everyone kissed goodbye, the two groups separated. Well, we went for the elevator to go out while the other guys stayed in.

"Oh my god, I can't believe this is my bachelor party!" I screamed inside the elevator. Thankfully there was no one else around. The guys all cheered.

As we spilled out of the elevator on the foyer level, I sidled up to Rory.

"The tiara becomes you," I said, squeezing his arm.

"I think so too."

"How was your walk with Sergei?"

He didn't meet my eyes, but he was smiling, which I thought was a great thing.

"It was okay. He's not as grumpy as he tries to pretend. I'll also never look at him the same way again after seeing him slurp a vanilla ice cream smoothie like a five-year-old that just discovered racing cars."

We all squeezed into a big cab, and Aiden gave instructions to the driver.

"Boys, may I say you all look fantastic tonight," I said.

"I'm glad you're all here, and I applaud your bravery at leaving your men behind. Who's ready to paint this town rainbow?"

Everyone cheered.

The cab stopped in front of a club like we were VIPs. The line to get in was enormous, and I hoped Aiden and Charlie had arranged some kind of fast-track entrance because there was no way we'd get in before the guys had to swap for the other party. It would be a shame for them to miss out.

Aiden spoke to the bouncer, and soon enough, we were being escorted inside.

The club was heaving, so we stuck together so we wouldn't get lost.

"Shall we grab a drink?" Rory asked. "The bar also seems the least busy area in this place." He was almost shouting to be heard over the music.

We made our way through the crowd until we reached the bar.

"Oh my god, Tom, you're glowing," Indy said.

"I know, right?"

Indy pulled my hand and started dancing with me right there. Ben joined, and soon the drinks we were going to have never got ordered. It must have been at least five songs before we stopped.

"Okay, now I really need a drink," Connor said.

"First round is on Charlie," Aiden said with a big smile, holding a black credit card.

The mention of Charlie gave me a pang of sadness. He was my best friend. He'd been there when my mom moved out of Boston. He entertained my level of crazy, and he had the biggest heart of anyone I knew.

"Hey," Connor said, putting his arm around me. "Rainbows aren't meant to be sad."

"I miss Charlie."

He gave me an understanding smile. "I know. Me too. Trust me, I'll kick his ass if he doesn't come up with a reasonable excuse for his absence. He better be ending world hunger or adopting some Lydovian child that needs a safe place to live."

I laughed at his words, and then it hit me. "Oh my fatherly god. That's it! Charlie and Kris are having a baby."

Aiden gave me my drink, and I took a sip, smiling at the sweet strawberry flavor.

"Sorry to break it to you, honey, but neither Charlie nor Kris can have babies," Connor said.

I elbowed him and said, "No, but what if they're adopting one? Let's face it, Charlie won't stop talking about the charity he created and the talented kids he's helping."

Connor smiled. "If anyone would do it, it would be my brother. Now, let's celebrate your night and give Charlie something to be jealous of when he hears all about tonight."

I raised my glass and shouted, "Let's dance!"

As the night went on, the DJ started mixing more pop songs into his tracks. It was as if I'd given him a list of my favorite tunes and he'd included them all in his set. I was buzzed, happy, and didn't think anything else other than ending the night with Wren inside me could be better.

"Guys, come this way. You will not believe this." Aiden and Ben had just returned from the restroom, so the guys immediately made a load of comments about getting lucky. As if they'd do anything like that. I'd bet my business that everyone was counting down the minutes to get to the guys in the suite.

We followed them until we reached a set of stairs to another floor.

"I swear to you if I'm kidnapped..." Rory said.

At the top of the stairs, there was a closed door. The door opened as we got to it, and a guy came out covered head to toe in glitter.

"Man, it's wild in there," he said.

We all looked at each other. The only one who seemed mildly panicked was Rory, but then he shrugged, so we all went in.

The guy's assessment was accurate, but the place wasn't just wild. It was *my* brand of wild.

"Is that Britney Spears?" Ben asked.

"Probably a tribute act," Indy replied.

"Is that a unicorn making out with a...tooth fairy?" Connor asked.

The singer was performing "Baby One More Time," but not the original version. Every time she sang *hit me,* the crowd went wild. She repeated the words over and over again until they started counting down.

When the count got to one, it started raining glitter.

A tear ran down my cheek.

"Hey, you okay?" Indy asked. I hadn't even noticed I was frozen in my spot.

"Guys," I said. "Welcome to the inside of my brain. I didn't realize I'd signed up for a CAT scan."

"Come on," Rory said. "Let's all be Tom for the next hour before we go back to the suite."

"I'll get the drinks," Aiden said.

"I'll help," Connor added.

Despite the crowd, we managed to carve out some space for our small group. We danced with each other, and at some point, we had a fairy godmother, a Peter Pan, and a Care Bear join us.

I let the music take me into my happy place and moved until it was time to leave.

I wondered what the night had been like for the other guys so far.

As soon as the guys left for their party, everyone else took a seat on one of the many couches we had in the lounge area.

The mood was definitely different without the other guys.

Slade stood up and went over to the bar. "I know you're all moping because your men are out there having fun, but even though we are exponentially more boring than them, we can still have a great evening. Who's up for a drink?"

It was raised hands all around.

The hotel team delivered a bunch of trays with sandwiches and snacks to the suite, which we put in the kitchen area. No doubt the guys would come back hungry.

I was expecting our party to be a little more subdued. It was fine by me. I'd rather spend an evening drinking beer and chilling with my friends.

"Hey, Wren, I heard someone say they saw the Marinos coach around town. Is it true?"

I coughed as my drink went the wrong way.

"Oh man, that would be awesome," Tristan said. "You think he's scouting?"

"What else? He's a bit far from San Diego, isn't he?" Tate added.

"That kid who got the full ride to UT, his dad came to the shop last week. I overheard him talking to Liam about how thankful he is to Wren for being such a great coach," Slade said.

"You know it," James said. "Wren was always the best at school, not just playing but giving other players tips on how to play better. Wouldn't surprise me if the Marinos want to poach him instead."

Five heads turned to me.

"No comment," I said and stood up to pour myself another drink.

"Hey, man, you know we're tight. We wouldn't tell anyone," Tate said. "We'd just be fucking proud of you. Sad to see you leave town though."

When he shut up, everyone looked at him and then me, as if they suddenly got it. I downed my drink and poured another one.

"Is this a bachelor party or a session with Oprah?"

A knock on the door ended the conversation.

Since I was already standing up, I went over to answer it.

I opened the door to find a tall, muscly guy, wearing a shirt that had to be at least three sizes too small.

"Can I help you?"

"Your entertainment for the evening is here, sir." The guy kept a straight face, and I must have been a little buzzed from the three drinks I'd had because I just laughed.

"You're not really my type, but come on in."

"Believe it or not, it's not the first time I've heard that," he said, and there was a hint of a smile. He had dimples. Cute.

"Guys, you can thank or kill Charlie, but it looks like we're getting strippers," I said.

"Sir, if you'd like to find a comfortable seat."

I went back to the couch while the stripper went straight for the sound system, connecting his phone to it like he'd done it many times before.

"Sergei, dude, you're the only one who can tap that tight ass. Do us proud," James said.

Sergei growled and said something like, "He's not my type," from between his teeth.

The music started with a low beat. The guy went over to the door and stood by it like a bodyguard, hands in front, legs set slightly apart, and staring forward.

"For a stripper, he really looks the bodyguard part. I should know," James said.

The beat of the music gave way to a tune, and then the front door opened again. The guy didn't move as three women dressed as naughty students came inside, dancing as they made their way toward us.

The couches were in a kind of semi-circle, so the girls gathered in the middle, dancing to the music.

I looked beyond the girls to Sergei, who was the only one who knew the plan for the party. He shrugged.

James and Tate were trying to contain their laughter, and Tristan was trying to avoid looking at the girls altogether.

Slade raised his hands as if to say he had nothing to do with it.

I was going to kill Aiden if this had been his idea.

"Hello, boys, we hope you liked our intro. I hear we have a groom in the room tonight," one of the women said, and the other two whooped.

She walked around looking at all of us in turn before stopping in front of Slade. "Well, hello, Daddy. I've been a naughty, naughty girl."

Slade closed his eyes and pressed his fingers over the bridge of his nose.

"I'm the groom," I said to relieve Slade.

The three women crawled to me. Two of them kneeled by my side while the third sat on my lap.

"Congratulations, handsome. Has your lovely bride left you all on your own tonight?" she pursed her lips. "Don't you worry. Chrystal, Channelle, and I will make up for her absence.

"His."

"What's that, honey?"

"My fiancé is a man."

She laughed. "Well, that's no bother. Hopefully, you can still appreciate a good dance routine. Maybe your friends over there will enjoy it too."

"I doubt it."

"I'm sorry, ladies," Sergei said. "There must be some confusion. We were expecting male dancers."

"Why would you want—oh." When the information registered, the girls all stood up. They looked at each other with visible disappointment and then at the guy by the door, who was on his phone.

He ended his call and came over. "I'm so sorry, gentlemen. There was some confusion. It seems the hotel upgraded your package. Problem is, we don't have a premium package for male dancers, so whoever took the booking just sent the girls instead. We'll be on our way now."

"Wait," I said. "Does this mean they won't get paid?"

The guy nodded.

"We'll take them," Tate said straight away.

"Yeah," Tristan agreed.

"Do you still want us to dance for you?"

I looked at the guys, and an idea hit me. "Would you be willing to teach us some dance moves?"

The three women smiled and said, "Yes."

I turned to the guy. "You can join us if you want. There are some non-alcoholic drinks in the kitchen. Must be a little boring standing there on your own while you watch them work."

He smiled. "No sir, Leslie—I mean, Chrystal—is my wife. Best job ever." He smiled, and his dimples came out again. Damn, the guy was cute.

"Dude. Awesome gig," James said, holding up his hand for a high-five.

The six of us learning dance moves turned out to be the most fun I'd had in a long time. Devon, who, as it turned out, had served in the military at the same time as James but in a different unit, changed the music to a slow country song.

"Shirts off, boys," Chrystal ordered. "Now don't be shy. No one's gonna bite you. Well, Chanelle might, if you ask nicely."

We all laughed, and soon there was a pile of shirts on the floor.

"Damn," Devon said. "I'm gonna have a complex with all you dudes and your abs."

Chrystal laughed. "Yeah, but you're the only one I'm gonna go home with."

My heart burst as she gave her husband a small kiss before turning back to order us around. "Okay, now feel the beat of the song. Hear that bass. Doesn't it tickle all the way down to your crotch? I want you to move your hips like you're playing with a hula-hoop in slow motion."

"That's right. Woo!" Channelle whooped.

We were practicing our turns when the door of the suite opened and the guys spilled in.

"I must be reeealy drunk," Tom said. "I'm seeing girls now."

"Nah, I see them too," Ben said. "Hey, get your hands off my husband." He walked over to Tristan and gave Chanelle a murderous look. "Heeey, baby. Guess who loves you?"

Tristan smiled. "You do?"

"That's right," Ben said before he leaned against Tristan, dancing to the song.

I walked over to the love of my life, who seemed to be a little more than just buzzed.

"Hey, Angel," I said. "Want a glass of water?"

He nodded. I walked him to the kitchen area and took out a glass and a bottle of water from the fridge.

"What's going on?" he asked.

"Our strippers were teaching us to dance."

He drank the full glass and then wiped his mouth with

the back of his hand. "I must be really drunk. I just heard you say you were learning how to dance from strippers."

"You heard right. And if you're lucky, I might give you a demonstration of what I learned later."

"You're on, big boy." He cupped my erection, and I couldn't help leaning into it.

"Come on, let's join the others. Maybe it's your turn to dance for us."

JAMES

I watched Connor as he held on to Rory by the door. They seemed to be engrossed in a conversation. Connor had his arm around Rory, who was just a little shorter.

When Connor and I first got together, I used to feel some jealousy toward Rory. After all, Rory had taken my place. He'd become Connor's best friend in my absence. He'd been there for the football games, the trips to Benny's, graduation, college. And I hadn't.

Now I knew that hadn't been the truth because no one had replaced me. Connor had missed me every single day we were apart. Keeping a Jamie-shaped space in his heart. Just like I'd done to him.

All those years that I'd lied to myself about how important his friendship had been to me when we were kids. But I guess the heart wants what the heart wants, and in my case, it was Connor.

My Connor.

The music in the room never stopped. Devon had

become our personal DJ, picking just the right kind of song. And as if he had a sixth sense for the mood in the room, he chose more upbeat poppy music.

Rory went over to the bar and fixed himself a drink. Connor looked around the room until he found me. His smile said more than a thousand words.

He came over and straddled me on the couch.

"Looks like we've interrupted an awesome party," he said, running his fingers down my naked chest. "I didn't realize this is how strippers at bachelor parties worked. Or you got seriously played."

I laughed. "Are you complaining?"

He ran his hands up my chest again and over my neck. "Hell no. You look perfect."

I put my hand behind his neck. His breath mixed with mine until our lips met in a kiss that was hot and full of promise.

"I want to make love to you tonight, Jamie."

"Yes," I moaned against his lips. He sucked my lower lip into his mouth and then released it with a pop.

"Fuck, I'm so hard for you right now."

"Ditto, baby, but we can't leave now. Aren't we meant to swap parties?" I asked.

Connor sat up and looked around.

"I don't think anyone's going anywhere now. Come on, let's dance."

I let him pull me into the dancing area we'd created by pushing the couches back.

"Give us some Christina, Devon. I'm a genie in a bottle, and I'm gonna let Wren rub me aaall the right ways," Tom shouted, and everyone laughed.

That set the mood to get everyone on the dance floor. Even Sergei was dancing and with one of the girls, nonetheless.

Connor turned around so he was dancing with his back to my front. I put my hands on his waist and let him move against me.

"Why are you all covered in glitter?" I asked.

"It was so mad, babe. We found this room at the club. There were unicorns, fairies, cartoon characters, anything you could think of. The music was awesome, and it rained glitter."

"You had fun?"

"Uh-huh."

Connor raised his arms and locked them behind my head. I kissed his temple and saw him close his eyes. We moved to the beat, side to side. I listened to the words in the songs. Everyone sang about love, but I wasn't sure they really knew what love was. Not like I did, at least.

I was lost in my thoughts when Connor turned around. His eyes met with mine, and I stared at those cute freckles he'd finally accepted.

"I'm ready if you are," he said.

"I thought you agreed we shouldn't leave so early."

"No, not that. The other thing."

I stopped. "You're sure?"

He nodded.

We'd been talking about having children, especially since Mary had been asking for grandkids since we got married, but it hadn't been the right time.

Connor still spent a lot of time working on our events business. He was the one who made the contacts and traveled to traders' conferences to learn about the latest finds in celebrations.

I just worked on anything that had to do with the house itself, which seemed to be a never-ending job.

We'd decided to wait a while and promised that as soon as one of us was ready, we'd tell the other, and then we'd talk about it. I never had any intention of saying no to Connor whenever he was ready.

"Do you remember that day when you were with your brother and sister arguing about the house?"

I nodded. The relationship between me and my step-siblings had improved greatly since then.

"That day, I went for a walk and met with Rupert. He was doing some work in the garden, so I tried to give him the seeds Ollie gave us. He said I needed to think carefully about where to plant them because I'd need to be around to look after them."

"I didn't know that."

He smiled. "When I looked up, I saw you by the window. You looked so lost, and my heart broke for you. For the little boy who was uprooted from his world and the adult who still had to face the consequences of someone else's life choices. I...I also saw a happy house, with cars parked outside, children running around. That was when I realized I was in love with you and nothing would ever make me feel differently."

"Oh, baby." I kissed him with all my love. When we stopped, I held him tight, and we slow-danced to our own tune.

Everyone else seemed to be doing the same. Aiden and Slade, Ben and Tristan, Tom and Wren. Tate was on the couch with Indy draped over him, drinking a large glass of water.

Sergei danced with one of the girls, and Rory seemed to be doing the same. He was probably the only guy here who'd have loved a personal dance from the girls. He and Wren, although I doubt Tom would allow that to happen.

"What are you laughing about?" Connor asked.

"About how nine gay men ended up in a bachelor party with three female strippers and their bodyguard."

"He's cute, right? Those dimples."

"Hey!"

"Don't worry, baby, you're the only bodyguard I'll ever want or need."

"Damn right. You think we should signal the guys to give Rory and his girl some space?" I asked.

"That's probably illegal, but they're consenting adults, so..." he shrugged.

I looked at Rory again. He had his eyes on Sergei, but when his girl twirled around him, he noticed me and placed his eyes right back on the girl.

Interesting.

I couldn't remember ever feeling like this. So free, uninhibited.

The beat of the pop music flowed through my veins, making me want to raise my arms above my head, move my hips, sway to the music.

There was part of me that wanted to let go completely. Shed the fake skin I'd been wearing all my life.

I had no reason to keep my secret. Since my dad retired from his job as a diplomat, I'd made it very clear to my parents that I would never be part of their show and tell again. I didn't want that life where I was set up with women or paraded like a show prize.

Our strained relationship became even more distant, but it was what it was, and I had made peace with my decision. Even without coming out, I already owned more of my life than ever before.

Maybe that's why I felt like I was one split-second decision away from blurting it out. I could own the last little piece of my life and be authentic.

I hugged Tom from behind as he danced with Wren.

"I fucking love you, man," I said to him. "You are the most authentic person I know, and one day, I will be brave too. I promise."

He turned around and gave me the smallest kiss on the lips and then a hug.

Somehow a tray with new drinks appeared on the coffee table, so I picked one and drank until I felt the alcohol burn my throat. I needed some water before I got too drunk.

I noticed Indy go toward the restroom, but when he came back, he didn't sit with Tate like I expected. Instead, he came over to me and held my hands.

We danced like that for a bit.

"All okay with you and Tate?"

"I might kill him before the night is over, but meh." He shrugged.

"Why's that?"

"He's killing my buzz. He made me drink all this water. I think I'm less drunk now than before we left to go to the club."

I laughed as he raised my hand and twirled before coming back to face me.

"This is a bachelor party. You're meant to get drunk and make poor choices."

His pout was quite sweet, especially because his usual messy bun was even messier.

"Anyway, let's dance."

After a couple of songs, Ben came over to us, followed by Connor, Aiden, and Tom. The rest of the guys went back to sit on the couch.

"Okay, guys, I need some advice," Aiden said, keeping

his voice low. "How do I convince Slade that we need another cat?"

Indy was the first one to contribute. "Didn't Harley just turn up? You thought she was his, and he had no clue that he'd just been adopted by both a kitten and the best-selling gay romance author in the country."

"True," Connor said.

"Okay, I'll speak to Micah when I go to pick up Harley. He might have a rescue in need of adoption.

"Speaking of which," Tom said. "There's a football game to raise money for Micah's charity on Monday night. Rory, we need you to play defense because one of the other players pulled his back. We have the offense covered. James is playing quarterback, but we need a solid defense."

I shook my head. "First question. Do you even know what you just said?"

"Not a damn clue," he answered.

"Why did Wren send you then?"

"Because I'm adorable, and you won't deny me." He batted his eyelashes and gave me a big smile.

"Fine, I'll be there."

"Dude, you're so weak," Aiden said. "Slade has managed to avoid joining the adult team for almost two years now. I thought you'd make it at least six months."

"Thanks for the warning, you fuckers," I said. "I'm going to dance with people that have my back, thank you very much."

I gave them the finger and turned around, almost bumping into one of the girls: Crystal or Channelle. They were both blonde and wearing the same outfit, so it was hard to tell.

"Hey, handsome," she said.

"Hi. Enjoying the party?"

"For sure. Best party I've ever worked," she said.

"These are all good guys. You girls are safe here."

She nodded. "I can tell. Everyone here's gay," she laughed.

"I'm not."

She laughed again. "You sure?"

I didn't know why I said it. I could have just not made a comment. Kept it open and undetermined. Usually, I kept things so close to the vest that I easily passed as straight. That and years of practice. There was really no need to affirm it.

"Why do you say that?"

She lifted her arms and started moving around me like she wanted to wear me like a second skin. Then she turned around and moved her hips to the music.

I put my hands on her waist to keep her from toppling over because she did this weird move where she bent all the way down and then back up.

Then she turned around and tightened her cropped shirt. My eyes followed her fingers as she ran them down the frilly top of her bra.

"Sweetheart, I've been doing this for a while. The only time a guy didn't get hard with me rubbing myself against him, he was seventy-four. Even then, I felt a little stirring in the poor guy's pants."

I opened my mouth, but no sound came out. I could feel my skin heating up.

"I'm sorry, did I overstep?" she asked with visible concern.

I shook my head. I glanced at the guys. There were only a few still dancing because Tom and Aiden had gone back to their fiancés.

"No...you're right. It's just..."

"I know." She put her hand on my arm. "My brother's gay. He's like this super-masculine guy into sports and cars. He really struggled to come out, especially to his friends, because he didn't know where he fit. He still likes all these macho male-associated things, but he just wants to be with a man rather than a woman. Only you can tell when you're ready. I'll keep your secret."

"That's the thing. I'm tired of keeping secrets. I feel like my skin is wearing really thin, and it's going to tear at any moment now."

"What's holding you back?"

Me. I wanted to say. I was the one holding myself back.

What was I scared of? All these men had come out at some point in the past, and they were still here, living their authentic lives.

"Excuse me," I said to her and went over to the bar.

I poured two fingers of scotch into a glass and drank it in one go.

"Fuck that burns."

It was now or never. I made a gesture for Devon to turn down the music and walked up to the group.

Everyone stared at me. Waiting.

"You okay, sweetie?" Tom asked.

I nodded. "I'm more than okay. I'm...I'm..." The words were stuck in my throat, but I couldn't go back now. "I'm gay."

Eleven faces stared at me in complete silence.

My heart was beating so fast I couldn't tell if anyone had said anything. My eyes met Connor's. He was frowning.

Suddenly, I felt like I was hyperventilating. I took a deep breath, but it didn't help.

"I'm sorry. I shouldn't have done that...I'm sorry."

I ran out of the room as fast as I could without looking back. If I could run to the moon, I would have, but I had to accept that my room was the closest place to hide in.

Everyone was in shock, including me. I'd suspected Rory was gay and very deep in the closet.

The way he wanted to look at me but forced himself to look away. I'd noticed it at Charlie's sister's wedding two years ago, and I'd seen it again over the last few days.

After our walk this afternoon and getting to know him, I figured a big part of the problem was probably his parents, but he was also likely worried about how his friends would react. I think he felt like he was lying to them, and they'd be hurt.

"Rory," Connor said with a pained voice.

Rory was gone and couldn't hear him, but I suspected the call was just a shock reaction.

"I need to see him," he said, standing up.

"Wait, Connor. I'll go."

He looked at me. "Why? He's my best friend. I should be with him right now."

I put a hand on his shoulder. "It's because you're his

best friend that you need to give him space. You're the one he thinks he hurt the most."

"Wait...you knew?"

I let out a breath. "I had an idea."

"How did I not know? How could I have missed it? He must have been in so much pain. Is it because of his parents?" Connor was mumbling and shaking his head. James pulled Connor back down to his lap and wrapped his arms around his husband.

"I'll go check on him, okay?"

I didn't wait for their reply before walking out the door and into the hallway. Rory was in the room next to mine, so I didn't have to go back down to reception to find out where he was.

I knocked on the door and waited.

No reply.

I knocked again. "Rory? It's me, Sergei. Please open the door. I just need to know you're okay."

No reply again.

I was going to call for him when the door opened slowly.

Rory didn't meet my eyes. His skin looked flushed as if he'd been crying.

"What do you want?"

"Can I please come in?" I asked.

"Why?"

"Because you're upset and probably need a friend right now."

He stepped away from the door but left it open.

"What I need is a hole to jump into." He was sitting on the bed, bent forward with his face in his hands.

I closed the door behind me and approached him carefully, kneeling in front of him on the carpet.

"Hey." I stroked his knee, glad he didn't move away. "What you did out there was really brave."

"It was stupid. I mean, who does that? Stop a party to announce they're gay?"

"There's no one way to come out. Let's face it, my coming-out story made it into the national papers. Imagine being caught holding hands with the boy you grew up with, just as you confessed to each other that maybe you had feelings beyond friendship."

He looked at me then. "I'm sorry. That must have been horrible."

"It was at the time, but it saved me having to come out over and over again. So there was a silver lining."

His lips turned up in a half-smile.

"Connor is going to hate me. I lied to him. Remember when I said I hurt someone? It was Charlie. I made him keep my secret and then I hurt him."

His eyes held so much pain I couldn't stop myself from touching his face. "Listen to me, Rory. There isn't a single person in that room who doesn't respect you and understand what you're going through. Yes, some may be surprised, but it doesn't mean they won't accept you."

He shook his head, but I held his face firmly so he could stare into my eyes. "Connor loves you. He's probably feeling guilty right now because he wants to be here to support you, but he's not angry or upset with you. He loves you too much for that. And I've never seen anything but concern for you from Charlie."

Rory stared at me as if he didn't believe my words.

"You were his friend at a time when he was hurting too. Remember? Every time I've been around Connor, every other word that comes out of his mouth is about you. Rory would love this. Maybe we should see if Rory is up for that. I haven't heard from Rory in a while, I wonder if he's okay. Rory. Rory. Rory. I swear to you, if James didn't know how much Connor loves him, he'd be jealous."

Rory smiled wider, but then his smile left him again.

"How about you? You don't look like you're surprised."

I smiled. "What can I say, Kitten. There was something about you when we met. You tried to protect me from James, even though you were this itsy-bitsy thing. I felt your breath hitch when I held you closer to stop you from getting hit if James really did come for me. At the time, I put it down to maybe holding you too tight, but then at the wedding, you were so quiet. You looked at people as if you were asking for permission to be there. And then there were your eyes. Those deep pools that you keep hiding from people, but not from me. I always saw you. All the layers, all your depth. So no, Rory. I didn't know, but...maybe I hoped."

Rory's hands came up to my face. I stood still, at risk of scaring him away. His hands were shaking, but his touch was soft.

He closed his eyes and then pressed his lips against mine.

All of the shields I'd raised to protect my heart were obliterated before I took another breath.

Rory opened his mouth and closed it again around my lips, this time pressing harder. I rose on my knees, which put us at a more even level and allowed him to take charge of the kiss.

I just hoped I'd get my turn because I wasn't leaving this room without having my fill of Rory. Not a chance.

He moved one leg around my back and pulled me even closer. I growled against his lips and put my arms around him, standing up and taking him with me.

"Yes," he rasped without taking his lips from mine.

I liked to think I was the fountain Rory was so thirsty to drink from, but even I knew this was likely a reaction to the chain of events.

Still, I didn't pull back. I didn't stop it.

Instead, I laid him on the bed and covered his body with mine.

His hardness was unmistakable. Pressing against mine, needing more.

"God, Rory, you're...fuck." I couldn't even form a sentence.

"Sergei, please."

"What, Kitten? What do you need?"

"I need you." His hands clawed at my shirt in a hurry to get rid of it. "You're so...ripped. When we walked into the suite, and I saw you shirtless, I nearly came right there and then. I was lucky that Connor was telling me about his pets, so I was able to focus on that, or my secret would have been out then."

I chuckled. "So you like what you saw, huh?"

"Very much."

"And what are you hiding under this preppy shirt?" I sat up on my heels, taking Rory with me. I pulled his shirt from his back and over his head. I swallowed as I took in his body. Rory didn't have much hair, only a small nest between his pecs and a delicious-looking trail going south from his belly button.

It was covered by his slacks, but I'd be revealing that as soon as I had my answer to something else.

"What does this mean?" I asked, tracing the Chinese characters he had tattooed on his chest just above his heart.

"It means *love yourself*. I got it in Singapore after I spoke to my parents. We'd been out at an event together. They set me up with the daughter of some diplomat. I didn't want to be rude, so I sat with her. She turned out to be really sweet. The first thing she said was that she wasn't interested in me. She had a boyfriend her parents didn't agree with, but she was in love. It was like a weight was lifted, and it turned out to be the best event I'd ever attended. We left the party together." He laughed. "I still remember the smiles on my parents' faces. Her boyfriend picked us up and took us to this late-night market. There was a tattoo parlor, and I decided to do it right there. I don't even know if the words mean what I think they mean. It could be an order for sweet and sour chicken for all I know."

It was my turn to laugh. "I like sweet and sour chicken."

"You do?"

"I like your mouth more. I like it when you're prickly, I like it when you're yourself, I like it when you smile. Especially your smile."

Rory stared at me and bit his lip. "Are you...are we...?"

"We are, Kitten. Anything you want."

I kissed his neck, sucking a patch of skin until I could

feel it raise. I didn't care. Rory was mine tonight, and we'd have that as a reminder, at least until I left.

"Can you make us both come with your hand?"

His question was so out of left field but so Rory at the same time. He was slowly peeling off his layers and showing me the real person beneath.

I removed our pants until we were naked. Once again, Rory took my breath away. The last person I needed to be thinking of right now was my ex, but he'd been right. Rory was the perfect match for me.

He was small, someone I could easily throw around, but he wasn't weak. The toned muscles on his stomach and his thighs showed me another layer of Rory.

"God, you're gorgeous."

I pushed him back on the bed and opened his legs so I could fit between them. His dick was hard and pointing up, begging to be touched.

His eyes bulged when he looked at my cock. I chuckled. "Yes, Kitten. I'm big all over."

"Ugh," he groaned, covering his face with his hands. "This isn't my first time, you know. I have some experience. But it's been a while, hence me behaving like an inexperienced teenager."

"I can live with that reaction to my cock, but I think I'd rather hear you moan my name."

I gave my cock a few strokes and then positioned myself on top of Rory.

We kissed and rutted until our breathing became more erratic, our need a lot more urgent.

I licked my palm and reached for our dicks between us. It was the most exquisite feeling. Having Rory under me, his orgasm dependent on how much pressure I placed on his cock, how fast I moved against him.

It was powerful and heady.

"Sergei...fuck, I'm close."

I kissed him harder until I was sure both our lips would come out bruised.

"Come on, Kitten. Come for me," I said into his ear. I sucked the lobe into my mouth and gave it a little bite.

Rory came with tiny moans that were barely audible. His warm cum gave me added lubrication, and with a few more strokes, I was coming on his stomach.

It took me a moment to gather my thoughts. I worried I was too heavy for Rory, but he just held me closer.

"Let me clean you up," I said.

I got up and went to the bathroom to grab a towel.

When I went back into the room, Rory was staring out the window. He smiled when I ran the wet cloth over his stomach but didn't say anything.

I wasn't sure what to do next, but he made that decision for me.

"Will you stay?"

"I will, Kitten."

"*B*abe, our room is the other way," Indy said.

"I know."

"Then why are you pulling me in the wrong direction?"

I was glad the party had wound down after Rory's confession because it was easier to get Indy out without having to make excuses.

Poor Rory. Coming out was never easy on anyone, but considering everyone thought he was straight, it looked like he'd had a particularly hard time either coming to terms with his sexuality or the coming-out part itself.

Because of my broken relationship with my dad, I'd never had a problem coming out. I'd done it hoping he'd hate me enough to send me back to my mom and Tristan, but he hadn't cared enough about me to make any kind of deal, big or small, about me being gay.

When the elevator hit our floor, a few people got out, so we managed to get in to go down.

"Tate?"

"We're just going on a little...adventure," I said, bringing his hand up and kissing the back of it.

He chuckled. "You know what happened the last time we were here, right?"

"I have vague memories."

He settled against my side as we rode the elevator down to the first floor.

Despite the late hour—or early depending on how you saw it—the hotel foyer was still busy. Vegas never slept, but differently to how New York never slept.

We approached the front of the hotel and waited for the next available cab.

"I'm still thinking about Rory," Indy said.

"I know, me too."

"I really had no idea. Not that I spent much time with the football players at school. Wren, Connor, and Rory were always a lot closer to each other. But to come out like this? Right now? He must be hurting a lot."

I held Indy tighter in my arms. "Thankfully, he has a big group of friends who will support him."

"True."

We took the next cab, and I showed the driver my phone to tell him where we were going.

"You really want this to be a surprise? I'm intrigued," he said.

I took his hand and settled it against my lap. The box in my pocket was burning a hole, and I hoped the car ride wouldn't be that long.

Of course, as soon as we pulled up at the chapel we got married in, he recognized it straight away.

"What are we doing here?" he asked.

"Definitely breaking Aiden's rule."

"Babe, in case you haven't noticed, we're already married. And we did it twice."

Oh, I'd noticed. Every morning that I got to kiss Indy before he went down to the bakery was a perfect morning. The start of a day in which I could call Indy my husband. A day that would end with him falling asleep in my arms.

A girl dressed like Marilyn Monroe came out to greet us.

"Welcome back, gentlemen. We're delighted that you decided to return to our little chapel to renew your vows." She looked around and then said in a lower tone, "I always wonder how long couples really last once they get out the door. Some you can tell will regret it before the sun is up."

Indy wrapped his arm around my waist, and I kissed his temple.

"The first time we did it, we were definitely one of those couples. But it seemed we were really destined to be together," I said.

"How romantic," she said, pulling a white handkerchief from the pocket of her dress and dabbing the corner of her eye. "I'm a sucker for real love stories. I really should move out of Vegas. Anyway, follow me. Since you don't need paperwork and you've settled the bill, we're ready for you."

The morning after we got married, we'd returned to the chapel to see if we could cancel it. We never made it farther than reception.

We stopped by the double doors leading to the ceremonial hall and faced each other.

"I can't believe we're doing this again," Indy said. "Is this why you were forcing me to drink water?"

"I want you to remember everything."

"I wasn't the one with the memory problem," he joked.

The doors opened, and the music started playing. We walked slowly up the aisle, occasionally looking at each other and smiling.

I'd requested witnesses, so it seemed today we had half the members of Backstreet Boys.

"Welcome, Tate and Indigo Brooks. We're delighted to celebrate with you the renewal of your vows. To celebrate your love for each other. You promised to love, honor, and cherish one another through it all. And while life has brought you both wonderful blessings and difficult challenges, here you are today, having fulfilled the vows to love, honor, and cherish each other. Tate, can you repeat after me..."

I stared into Indy's dark-blue eyes, and the world disappeared. I repeated the words the officiant told me to say, but they weren't even close enough to how I felt about my commitment to Indy.

"Now would you like to say your own vows?" the officiant asked.

"I didn't bring any," Indy said, his eyes watering.

I ran my thumbs over his eyes to clear them.

"It's okay, baby. I wanted to make a promise to you tonight. Indy, you're the most special person I've met in my entire life. You're beautiful inside and out. When I didn't think I could be more, you showed me I could. You didn't change me. You showed me I'd always been this way. Capable of loving and being faithful because there will never be another man for me. Not in this lifetime or the next."

Indy's lip trembled, and I held him in an embrace.

"Indy, we're about to embark on the next stage of our lives as parents. Our little boy will know nothing but unconditional love. If he's anything like you, he'll be the most perfect little boy. If he's anything like me? Well...I apologize in advance. We may want to rethink buying that place with the treehouse."

Indy laughed but didn't move away from my arms.

"I know you will be up early, you will sleep late, you will learn everything you need to make sure our boy is cared for. My promise to you today is that I will be right there with you every step of the way. We will be a true partnership when it comes to loving and caring for our boy, but we will also not lose what we are to each other. You are also my lover, and there isn't a single time you walk into a room without causing an effect on me. I know that won't change ever...Indy Brooks, I love you, and I promise again to cherish and look after you for the rest of our lives."

Indy sobbed quietly against my chest. I could almost feel him cursing me in his head. Then he inhaled deeply and looked into my eyes.

"I have no words that can express how much you mean to me, Tate. I know you're scared and worried about the future. I am too. But I know we can do it because together, we are stronger. There is no one else I wish more to be a parent with than you. Because I know you'll teach our child all the things I can't. Together we will offer the balance that maybe wasn't always present in our lives. I promise to love you and cherish you for the rest of our lives."

My eyes watered, but I took a deep breath to keep my

tears at bay. I reached into my pocket and took out the little box.

"What's this?" he asked.

"We already have rings. They're just for us. I thought that if we had a chain around our neck, we could keep adding to it as our family expands."

He opened the box, and inside were two thin platinum chains, each with two charms. One to symbolize our love and one to welcome our first child.

"These are beautiful, Tate."

I put one around his neck, and he put the other around mine.

The officiant cleared his throat. "When you walk out of those doors, don't forget the promises you made here. Go live the rest of your lives in happiness."

Someone holding a camera took a few photos of us, and minutes later, we were back in a cab to return to the hotel.

As soon as we were inside the room, Indy took his shirt off and came for mine.

"That was the most beautiful thing, Tate. I still have no words, so I plan on showing you exactly what tonight meant."

"Oh yeah?"

"Uh-huh."

My eyes went to the back of my head when he palmed my erection while sucking one of my nipples and then the other.

"Bed," I growled.

He removed all his clothes in seconds and jumped on the bed, bouncing a little before I followed him, covering his body with mine.

The gentle touch on my cheek brought me back from my dream. I was in a field and there were flowers everywhere. I felt so peaceful that I didn't want to leave.

"Rory."

I opened my eyes slowly to adjust to the light. I remembered falling asleep staring out the window with Sergei holding me from behind.

But it wasn't Sergei's face that I saw when my eyes focused.

"Connor."

"Hey, honey."

I rubbed my face with my hands and burrowed under the blanket with a groan.

"How did you get in?" I asked.

"Sergei let me in."

"Where is he?"

"My guess is his room unless he planned on going down to breakfast in his boxer shorts."

"Oh god," I groaned from under the covers.

Connor lifted the covers and joined me underneath.

"I have so many questions, but the main one is, are you okay?"

I let out a breath. "You mean after I spectacularly came out to everyone?"

"Ask Indy one day how he came out to his parents," he chuckled. "But seriously."

"I'm okay...I think. I feel embarrassed more than anything. Connor, I never meant to lie to you."

"You didn't because you don't owe me or anyone your sexuality. I know how it feels, remember? I was almost engaged to a woman and never gave guys a second thought. I guess my James-sexuality was dormant until he came back into my life."

"You don't think you're gay or bi?" I asked.

"I don't know. Never gave it much thought. I can appreciate a good-looking man and a good-looking woman, but no one has ever stirred any kind of feelings in the same way just looking at James through the window does. To me, it doesn't matter because I'm happy. And all I want is for you to be happy too."

I nodded.

"Are you happy, Rory?"

"I don't know. I've been working myself up to this moment since I came back from Singapore. I nearly did it that day we met in Stillwater, but then we were interrupted, so I chickened out."

"Are you going to come out from under the covers? The guys are meeting up for breakfast, and they all want to see you."

"Ugh, no, can I stay here?"

"I'm not sure you have a choice. They might need coffee first, but they're working on their late-blooming jokes already and may break down your door."

I snorted. "I'm not a late bloomer."

"Didn't think you were."

"Connor..." I closed my eyes. "I hurt Charlie a lot."

"What do you...wait...?"

Even under the semi-darkness of the covers, I saw him thinking about what I'd just said.

"Charlie was my first boyfriend. My first everything. I knew it was wrong to be with him in secret. He deserved so much better. I was a coward and couldn't bring myself to end it. After he went to college, I made it look like I'd been with other guys, so he broke up with me. Two years ago, when my dad announced he was retiring, I thought I finally had a chance with him. I tried to tell him, but I made a mess of it. It worked out because he met Kris, and they're definitely meant to be together."

"You were heartbroken. Is that why you left?"

I nodded. "I already had some job offers I intended to decline, but I couldn't be around you or your family when I was like that. Everyone would have asked questions."

"I'm really sorry that happened to you, Rory. I wish I'd have known. That I could have been there for you, but I was facing my own life clusterfuck."

I shrugged. "It was what it was. It's taken me a long time, but the only way I could go back home was when I accepted that my actions had a part to play in Charlie and Kris's love story, and yours a little too. That made me feel less bad."

"But you still didn't accept yourself, did you?"

"No. That was the hard part."

Connor shuffled under the covers, pulling me into his chest.

"You know I'm naked, right?" I asked.

"Are you hard?"

"No."

"That's okay then. Now tell me why Sergei ran after you last night and was still here this morning."

I stayed quiet. I didn't know exactly what had happened. Maybe there was a mutual attraction that had been bubbling since we met, went away, and resurfaced when he came back.

Memories of last night flooded my brain. The way his heavier body pinned mine in place. The way he commanded my pleasure, took control, and let me just feel.

"Okay, I can feel you getting hard now, and it's weird. I'll take a wild guess and say the Lydovian Viking did a good job last night," he laughed, and I pushed him away.

I sat up in bed, making sure to cover my junk.

"So...?" he nudged me.

"I'm not gonna tell you what happened if that's what you're asking for."

"I don't want details, thanks. But I want to know what it means because if I need to round up the troops to give him a good kick, I will."

I laughed. "Thanks for wanting to protect my virtue." I sighed. "I don't know what it meant for him or for me. I was in a vulnerable place last night, and he gave me what I needed. Maybe we would have talked about it this morning. And maybe I would have woken up with him sucking my dick, but I'll never know because your mug was the first thing I saw when I woke up."

He laughed out loud. "Sorry for cockblocking you."

"I need a shower," I said.

"Go ahead. I'll wait."

I rolled my eyes and got up.

"You have a hickey on your ass cheek," he gasped.

"Really?" I looked in the bathroom mirror, and there it was.

I jumped in the shower before the water was even warm enough because the thought that I'd been so horny and desperate for Sergei that I hadn't noticed him sucking on my ass made me hard. With Connor in the room, there was no way I could do anything about it.

Fifteen minutes later, we joined the guys in the restaurant.

I wasn't sure what to expect, but getting a hug from every one of them was not it.

Sergei was the last one. My body reacted immediately as he whispered in my ear, "You okay?"

I gave him a small nod before taking my seat. "So, what's good here?"

There were a couple of snorts around the table as the couples looked at each other.

"Okay, okay, let's release the elephant. I'm sorry about my little coming-out show, but here we are. I'm glad I don't have to pretend anymore."

My eyes met Tom's, and he smiled at me, mouthing *so proud*. I smiled back.

Who knew I'd strike up such a great friendship with my ex's best friend?

"So, what happened after I left?" I asked.

"We're adopting another kitten from Micah," Aiden said. Slade just shook his head, clearly having been played by his fiancé.

"We decided we're ready for children now, so we're going to start the process of looking for a surrogate," James said.

I looked at Connor, who had a loved-up smile.

"Dibs on godfather," I said, and Connor gave me a one-armed hug.

Ben looked at Tristan, who nodded. "We're having a baby. Ellie called this morning to say she's pregnant."

"We're really excited to give Charlotte a half-sibling," Tristan said.

Tate reached out to give his brother a fist bump. "What you guys are doing for each other is really sweet. I'm sure the kids will appreciate growing up with a sibling, even if they have different parents...well, one of the parents."

Indy hugged Ben, who was sitting next to him, and then said, "We renewed our vows last night in the same chapel we got married in the first time."

There was a collective gasp, and then Tom stood up, holding his hand out and wiggling his fingers. "Pay up, suckers."

We all took our wallets out. Even Sergei.

"Wait up, you had a bet on us renewing our vows?" Tate asked.

Aiden shook his head. "I was really hoping you'd take my warning seriously. I'm going to have trust issues from now on."

"How about the grooms?" Ben asked.

Tom looked at Wren like he hung the moon and the stars. "Surprisingly, all we did was make love until the sun came up in the sky, and then we took a nap. This weekend was really the best, guys. I don't want to get too emotional, but we couldn't have asked for a better bachelor party. I mean, who else would have a drill sergeant instead of a dance instructor or spend the bachelor party dancing with the wrong kind of strippers?"

Wren raised his coffee cup for a toast, and everyone cheered.

I was glad they didn't ask me how my night went because I hadn't had enough coffee yet to trust my running mouth.

"Okay, guys," Aiden said. "Since we're not bound by the constraints of commercial flying, you all have the day to yourselves. We'll meet in the lobby at four."

Most of the guys agreed to meet in the pool and then have lunch together at the pool restaurant.

I looked at Sergei since he'd been quiet. His nod was almost imperceptible, but I got his message.

Connor turning up at Rory's room had definitely changed my plans for the morning, but it had probably been for the best.

I'd had time in my room to grab a shower and think about last night. Not that anything had become any clearer. I was just hornier from all of my Rory-filled thoughts.

As the guys finished their breakfast, they left the table to go back to their rooms to change into their swimming trunks or get ready to go exploring.

I left the restaurant through the exit leading to the hotel gardens with Rory right behind me.

We stopped by the fountain. The need to touch him was too strong, so I broke the distance between us and cradled his face with my hands.

"How are you feeling this morning?" I asked.

"I'm...good."

"I'm sorry for leaving you. I thought you might need some time with your friend."

He nodded. "Thank you."

"Trust me, if Connor hadn't knocked on the door, you would have woken up in a vastly different manner."

His smile was everything, and I stopped resisting its pull. When my lips touched his, he put his hands on my waist, gripping my shirt tight.

"Did you have a good chat?" I asked when our kiss ended.

"I told him about Charlie. He took it surprisingly well."

"Are you surprised?"

"Not anymore. I should have trusted him."

I ran the backs of my fingers over his cheek. Layer after layer of pain and secrets was being shed. I liked this Rory.

"Do you want to go for a walk?" I asked.

He shook his head.

"Join the others in the pool?"

He shook it again.

"Shopping?"

Another shake.

"Casino?"

I smiled, wondering how many wrong guesses I could get away with until my kitten asked for what he wanted.

"Can we go back to my room? Maybe you can show me how you wanted to wake me up this morning."

I took his hand and dragged him to the nearest elevator. On the way up, I peppered Rory's neck with kisses until he was shivering under my touch. He was so responsive. So needy for my touch.

If only he knew how desperate I was for him too.

His hands shook as he tried to open the door with the key card.

"Ugh, I can't," he said. "You're distracting."

"If you want me inside your tight little hole, then focus, Kitten. Or maybe you want to fuck me instead."

"Fuck." He leaned his forehead against the door.

I heard voices coming from around the corner of the hallway, so I took the key card from Rory's hand and opened the door.

As soon as we were inside, I closed the door and pushed him against it, claiming his mouth. I used my leg to open his, and he started riding my thigh.

I loved his little moans. It was as if he couldn't help himself.

I turned him around and put his hands against the door, kissing his neck and sucking a new patch of skin.

"You are so responsive, kitten. You want this so much."

"Yes."

I reached over for his cock and felt the hardness. He groaned when I stopped, but my goal was something else.

He was wearing loose jeans, so I didn't even have to unbutton them to drag them all the way down to his feet. He stepped away from them and opened his legs.

"Jesus, fuck." This man was perfect. His little round butt had a jiggle I'd been acquainted with last night but definitely not for long enough.

I bit his cheek and then licked over the mark I left there last night.

"Please, Sergei," he begged.

I put my hands on each cheek to open them up and licked a path from his balls up to his crease. He shook as I paid attention to his pucker, licking and sucking it until I could tell he was close to coming.

"No," he complained when I stopped.

I stood up and bit his earlobe. "I want you relaxed, baby, but it's too early to end this. I'm going to savor you like a gourmet dish."

He turned around and started removing my shirt. I let him. Last night we'd gotten too intense, too quickly. I wanted to see what Rory would do to me, given the chance.

He pushed me until the back of my knees hit the bed. I sat down, but he put a knee between my legs to encourage me to move up the bed.

"It's my turn now." He peppered my chest with kisses, moving down slowly.

He fumbled with the buttons on my jeans until he managed to get them undone so he could pull them down and out.

"You're so big, Sergei. I'm going to love having you inside me. Filling me up."

He licked my length over my underwear before he pulled it down enough to expose the head. He opened his mouth and sucked it so tight I thought my head was going to explode.

"Christ, Rory."

"Yes, call my name. I love it when you call my name."

"Argh." I lay down, trying not to come too soon because my kitten coming out of his shell would be my undoing.

He took more of my dick in his mouth until all I could hear was his slurping noises.

"Rory, baby. You need to stop that if you want me inside you."

He stood up and ran to the bathroom. I took the

opportunity to take a deep, calming breath and get rid of my underwear.

Rory came back with condoms and lube.

"Hoping to get lucky?" I asked.

His face took a serious turn.

"I used to keep them for hookups. Since I couldn't be with anyone in public, I sometimes picked up guys in hotel bars when I was traveling or occasionally in clubs. It's been a long time though. I'm surprised these are still in date. I'm negative just so you know. I used to test regularly, but it's been such a long time, I haven't needed it."

I pulled him down to lie on me and kissed him. "It's okay. You don't need to justify it to me. For the record, I'm negative too. Kris is the only guy I've ever been with."

"Really?"

"Does that surprise you?"

"Yes. I mean, no. I guess you're quite busy with your job. It's just that you're so...beautiful, strong. I thought you'd have a line of guys fighting for your attention."

I grabbed the lube and squirted some onto my fingers. I reached out to his crease, loving when he closed his eyes as I sought out his hole.

"Having willing guys and being willing to be with them are two completely different things, baby."

He bit his lip as he started pushing back on my fingers. The moving of his hips was also doing a number on my cock, which was sliding against his between us.

"Why me?" he asked.

"I don't know."

That was the truth. I didn't know why Rory and not one of the many men that had made themselves available to me. Some even offered to keep things a secret. But the problem was that I didn't want to be anyone's secret, and I didn't want anyone to stay hidden for me.

"Open your legs more. Straddle me," I said.

He did, but he sat up on my legs instead. I stared at the tight muscles on his stomach. His cock standing hard and pointing slightly upward.

I wondered how it would feel to have it hit my prostate over and over again.

Rory covered my cock with the condom and added a little more lube to it. Then he raised his hips and moved forward, lining up my cock with his hole.

He kept his hand on my chest as he lowered himself down slowly.

Those damned cute noises he made were going straight to my dick, and with the heat and tightness of his ass, I was going to burst at any moment.

Rory opened his eyes as he bottomed out. I could tell he was waiting for the pain to subside and give way to the wonderful feeling of being so full inside.

I stroked his cock, and he raised himself up a little and then down again.

As his pace increased, I felt myself walking a tightrope that was going to snap.

"Sergei...I need more...not like this..."

Thank fuck.

I held him by the waist and dragged us to the bottom of the bed. When I felt the carpet under my feet, I stood up. I was going to lower him down to the bed, but the guttural sound he made as he impaled himself on my cock even more made me stay in place.

He wrapped his arms around my shoulders and his legs firmly around my waist. I put my hands on his butt and fucked him standing up. I'd never done this before, but it was something I'd always wanted.

I grunted as Rory kept going, asking for more. I wasn't even sure who was in charge, but it didn't matter because we had the same goal.

"So good...fuck, fuck, your dick is so good," he said between gasps. "Jesus fuck, right there. That's the spot."

I laid him on the edge of the bed so I could release one hand to stroke him. In that position, with my feet still firmly on the carpet, I thrust hard and fast. My body took control until all that could be heard were grunts, heavy breaths, the slap of skin on skin.

"Sergei, I'm gonna come," Rory warned only half a second before he spilled into my hand, his body shaking uncontrollably.

I let go, too, filling the condom until there were stars behind my eyes.

We were sticky and sweaty and more than orgasmed out.

"Shower?" I asked, but I knew I didn't need to.

Rory was so relaxed he didn't move while I pulled out and removed the condom and then carried him to his bathroom.

We spent the rest of the day in Rory's room. We missed lunch with the guys and ordered room service instead. An hour before we were due to leave, I realized we hadn't even packed.

"This place is a mess," I said.

"Your fault."

I kissed him until he was a soft noodle. "We need to pack."

He nodded. "Sergei..."

"Yeah?"

"Can we...do you think we can...um...keep this between us?"

I should have seen it coming, but it still hurt.

"Sure."

I kissed his nose, got dressed, and went back to my room.

Flying on a private jet was definitely an experience. Even my parents, with all their connections, had never managed to do it.

I didn't know why that made me a little happy, but it did. Maybe it was because I didn't need to suck up to anyone or make friendships out of interest or with a goal in mind.

This wasn't something I'd sought. It had just happened. I'd be just as happy flying commercial.

After we took off and it was safe to move around, everyone went over to the middle part of the jet, where there were comfy couches and armchairs. Enough for everyone to claim a space.

Petra, the flight attendant, served us coffee and pastries. There was also a fruit basket that looked so amazing I wasn't sure it was made with real fruit.

The only problem was...Sergei.

He picked a seat farthest away from me, and when everyone moved to the lounge, he stayed where he was.

Indy tried to get him to join us, but he excused himself with work, pulling out his laptop from a case.

Connor noticed and looked at me, but all I could do was shrug.

"Man, what a weekend. I feel like I need another two days off just to recover," Slade said.

"Try having a four a.m. wake-up call tomorrow," Indy said.

"There's a difference between waking up at four and getting up at four," he replied, and Aiden blushed.

The guys ribbed them, making jokes about Slade's age and having to keep up with Aiden.

"Is there still much to do for the wedding?" Ben asked.

Tom waved his hand, settling so much further into Wren, it was as if he was trying to merge. "I'm not giving the wedding one single thought until we land."

"Liar," Wren said. "He's already checked his list...twice."

"Like Santa?" Tristan said.

"You try pulling off a Christmas wedding and then tell me how it goes," Tom muttered.

"Jeez, I totally forgot it's nearly Christmas," Ben said.

"Don't know how, baby. You can't walk a few yards around town without bumping into a Christmas tree, a Santa, or an Elf."

"I know what you mean," Indy said. "We're changing the menu to Christmas bakes this week, but I've been so focused on the baby that I even forgot about the season."

"Don't you all worry. Coming into our wedding will be like stepping into a magical Christmas fairy unicorn kingdom...but classy, of course," Tom said.

Connor raised his hand. "I can vouch for that since I've already got a million black Christmas trees in storage, a gazillion decorations, and a bunch of new hires who I'm not sure are happier having work over Christmas or seeing this wedding in real life."

The guys carried on talking about Christmas and the wedding. I switched off from the conversation and focused on Sergei.

He was frowning at his laptop. I couldn't see him typing anything, so maybe he was concentrating on reading something.

It was strange, but he looked a lot more like the Sergei I first met. The sweet, understanding, and sometimes commanding man I'd been with earlier today wasn't on the flight.

I stood up and went to the restroom at the back of the plane. The one at the front was closer to me, but that's not where I wanted to go.

Sergei didn't look up as I walked past him.

What the fuck's wrong?

Doubt and panic started rising in my chest. I looked at myself in the restroom mirror. The guy staring back was definitely not the same one that had boarded the flight two days ago.

I wanted to figure out things with Sergei, but I knew that whatever happened, I was now a free man. I smiled.

The guys seemed distracted with their conversations, so I took the seat next to Sergei. A quick glance at his screen, and I saw he was looking at a blank page.

"Writer's block?"

"What?"

I pointed at the screen.

He closed the laptop and looked out of the window. It was dark outside, so I could see his expression.

"Is everything okay?" I asked. "Why aren't you up there?"

"I'm working."

I snorted. "Oh really? On what? Digital origami?"

The corners of his mouth curled up a bit, but it lasted less than a second.

"You should go back to your friends. Word might get out. They can sniff sex a mile away, and this is a small jet."

"What exactly is this about, Sergei?" I asked, now getting angry at his attitude.

"Nothing. It's about nothing."

"Well, fuck you and your nothing. You can go back to staring at your blank screen and brooding." I stood up and went back to one of the other seats facing forward. I reclined the back and put a blanket over me.

Hopefully, the guys would think I wanted to sleep instead of seething in anger.

Stupid fucking gorgeous bastard. Who did he think he was? Just because he had a perfect dick and a perfect chest... and abs...and ass.

I must have fallen asleep because Connor woke me up for the second time today, telling me to sit up because we were landing.

Sergei stayed on the plane after everyone disembarked, which was just as good because I didn't want to look at him a moment longer than I had to.

Before we walked out of the small terminal of the private airport, Connor announced he needed the restroom. Then he pulled me by the hand and dragged me along.

"What? Just because I'm out now doesn't mean we need to get any closer. I'm not into watching other guys pee," I said.

"What the hell's gotten into you?" he asked.

"Nothing."

He gave me a look that said he wasn't buying it.

"It's been a long weekend. I'm emotionally drained. What do you want from me?"

He sighed and narrowed the space between us, giving me a hug.

"Sergei and I...I don't know. He's acting weird. Like he doesn't even know me. He was balls deep inside me hours ago, and now he's avoiding me," I said against his puffy jacket.

"Wow. I wasn't expecting...this will take some adjustment."

"What?"

"You, speaking gay."

I chuckled. "I've always spoken gay, just not to you."

"Honey, are you sure you're reading into it right?" he asked.

"I don't know how else to read it. When he left my room to pack, we were good. He's barely even looked at me since we all met up in the lobby to go to the airport. Not to mention he stayed away from everyone for the whole flight."

Connor sighed. "Yeah, that was weird. I'm sorry, honey. I wish I could make it better for you. I thought you guys had a connection."

I shrugged. "So did I."

"His loss. Come on, let's get out of here. Want to share a cab with us? We're stopping at Micah's to pick up Donny, Bubbles, and the kids."

I snorted. "I hope you realize how crazy you sound when you talk about your pets."

"Just because you killed your only goldfish—" He choked when I grabbed him in a headlock.

"Uncle!"

MICAH

I felt myself blush as I read Santi's message on my phone.

Santi: Can't wait to get home. I'm going to read your body like a book in braille...but I'm going to do it with my tongue.

I was so proud of how far Santi had come in accepting his condition. Of course, Santi being Santi, he was never many degrees of separation from some innuendo or dirty joke.

The problem was when the innuendo was a promise. It was really difficult working with a hard-on. Also, not professional.

"Doctor Sawyer," April called from the door. "Would you like help with the pets?"

"No, that's okay, April. You can go home if everything's done at the front."

"It's all done out front," she said. "I'll head home then. It's my granddaughter's birthday tomorrow, so I'm baking her a cake."

"That's great. Happy birthday to her then. Let me know if you need some time off for a party or something."

April came over and gave me a hug. "You're too kind for your own good. I'm glad you have your man to balance you out."

I laughed. "What's he done this time?"

"He offered to take me on a date if I keep George for the weekend."

I shook my head. "I hope you declined his offer. I mean, I know he's pretty irresistible, but I wouldn't wish George on anyone."

She laughed. "Too late. I figured you two could use some time together without a play-by-play recount from a parrot."

"Make sure he puts out on your date. He gives good hugs, and you want to see his abs."

"Doctor," she said, feigning horror but winking at me before disappearing to get her stuff.

I looked at tomorrow's calendar briefly before shutting down the computer. The guys had my private cell, so they'd call when they arrived to pick up their pets.

Once I had the consultation room cleaned, I took a quick shower and got dressed in jeans and a Christmas sweater. I'd asked my mom to knit this one especially for me, and it had arrived in the mail today. I couldn't wait to show it to Santi.

I went out to the back and through the dog's playpen to

the main sanctuary building. The volunteers that came in daily to help out had all gone home already, so it was just me and the dozens of animals that, for some reason, hadn't found their forever home yet.

Those and my own brood of unruly heathens.

I opened the door to the old barn and looked at the whiteboard. On one side, there was a list of chores and what had been done by the volunteers. On the other it said: *It has been 5 days since Olive plotted a great escape.* Underneath it said: *It has been 10 days since Olive brought in a new pet.*

Ten days. That was the longest time. Surely we were overdue for a kidnap. I should drop the neighbors a message.

"Okay, guys, almost home time," I said, approaching the cat's playpen but stopped when I saw the door open. "Fuck."

I looked around the barn, even inside the dog houses, and couldn't find them. Surely they wouldn't go outside with how cold it was.

What if they did?

I ran back to the practice to the room where I kept Donnie and Bubbles. The pair wouldn't be separated, and Bubbles needed to be in a turtle tank. I was already familiar with her escapee tendencies.

"Baby?" Santi called.

"In the back," I said, opening the door to the room and finding it empty. Well, almost. Bubbles' baby turtles were swimming happily, not bothered about their missing mummy. "Ugh, why?"

"What's up, gorgeous?" Santi came up from behind me

and wrapped his arms around my waist. "Hmm, you smell so good."

"It's shower soap and stress. The ideal pheromone combo."

He laughed. "What's Olive done now?"

Now that made sense.

"You're right. This has Olive written all over it."

"What does?"

"Harley and Coco are missing, and so are Donnie and Bubbles. The guys should be here soon to pick them up, and I can't find them. Already looked in the barn."

Santi ran his hands up and down my arms before turning me around. "They'll be here somewhere. We can look in the new building. It's not heated, but it's finished, so maybe they went there to get away from the other animals. Steve snores really loud."

I chuckled. Steve was a rescue donkey that had been abandoned in someone's field, probably hoping he'd be taken in. The field owner was elderly and couldn't take on another animal, so they brought him over to me.

"But first things first," he said, his voice taking a lower gravelly tone that caressed me from the inside out.

"Oh yeah?"

"Uh-huh." He pulled me closer and kissed me until my whole world was Santi and his mouth.

"Hmm, Santi...Jesus...why can't you kiss like normal people?"

"Because, baby, you consume my thoughts all day long. It's distracting. Think of it as payback. Besides, life's too short for *meh* kisses." he said.

I sighed, resting my head against his chest. "I like your payback. But we need to focus on the pets."

"By the way, what are you wearing? It's so soft," he said.

"It's an early Christmas gift for you. I'll show you later."

"Okay. Do you want to check the new building while I look upstairs?"

"Okay."

Santi's vision had deteriorated significantly in the last two months after we thought it may have stabilized for a while. He'd gotten used to keeping his eyes closed or wearing dark glasses to avoid straining his eyes.

I ran over to the new building, praying I'd find the runaways. I couldn't live with myself if I had to deliver bad news to my friends. As it was, I was already going to deliver some unexpected news.

The new building was empty. I cursed aloud before going back into the main house. I heard Santi as I went up the stairs, so I picked up my pace.

"Are they here?" I asked before I got to the top.

"See for yourself," Santi said.

He leaned against the kitchen counter and pointed toward the spare room.

I took a deep breath and went in.

"Fuck my life."

Olive raised her head and growled before lowering it down again on the bed. Gus and Alfie were settled against her belly, both asleep.

Donny was on Olive's spare bed, the one we kept in the apartment for when she came to work with me, and Bubbles was on his back.

Harley was curled up on the opposite end of the bed to Olive, with a kitten also asleep between her paws. "Jesus Christ," I muttered.

Coco was, of course, on top of the chest of drawers staring at me like she was supervising the group. I pointed at her. "I expected more from you, Mrs." She didn't even acknowledge me.

I went back out to the kitchen. "Where's George?"

"In our bedroom. It seems he has a quota of how many new friends he can hang out with at once."

I rubbed my temples. "There's a new kitten."

"I guess that board in the barn needs updating," Santi laughed.

I shook my head.

"I'm going to round them all up for their parents," I said.

"I'll get dinner started."

Not long after, the guys all came in talking about the weekend. I was only a little jealous of missing out on what sounded like a great time, but once a month, I worked an extra weekend, and it happened to fall on this one.

Bubbles, her kids, and Donnie were all in their travel cages, so I handed them to James and Connor first since they had a longer journey home.

Then I turned to Aiden and Slade.

"We have a little issue with Harley," I said, rubbing the back of my neck.

"Oh my god, is she okay?" Aiden asked in a panic.

"Everything's fine, but Olive found a stray kitten, and Harley won't let go. You should have seen her attitude when I tried to check the kitten for a tag."

Aiden beamed and then looked at Slade, who shook his head.

"We were actually going to ask if you had any kittens that needed a home because we were thinking of adopting one."

"For real?"

"Yeah."

I laughed. "Well, I guess your choice is made for you because seriously, Harley has claimed the poor thing. He's a boy, so we'll need to look at options when he grows up unless you don't mind having more kittens."

"Oh, hell no," Slade said.

"He's in good health, and I managed to clean him up. If you bring him back during the week, I can do a full check, register, and tag him. I'm sure you're dying to go home."

They left in a cab, and then there was one more left.

I brought Coco out in her carrier and sat with Tom and Wren in the reception area.

"Um, guys...so..."

They stared at me, which I thought was a much better reaction than Aiden's.

"Did you know Coco is pregnant?"

"What?" they both said at the same time.

"I didn't notice it when you brought her in because she was in a mood and wouldn't leave her carrier, but when she saw Harley, she came out to play. Initially, I thought something else was wrong, but nope, she's just pregnant. Looks like you're set to be parents in the new year."

Tom and Wren stared at each other for a long time. Until Tom threw himself into Wren's arms. "We're going to be dads!"

Wren held Tom close. "It looks like it."

"Okay, we need a list of things to do. And research. Oh my god, she's going to need a bigger bed, and—"

"Babe," Wren said. "We'll work through it. Let's just go home first, okay?"

"Okay."

I closed the door behind them and joined Santi upstairs.

"All good?" he asked.

He was on the couch with a textbook. I took it from his hands and straddled him.

"Yeah. I'm starving. What have we got? Smells nice here."

"Pasta bake. It's in the oven, so we have time to make out."

I laughed. "Sounds like a plan." I leaned over and kissed him. It was unrushed. Just us teasing and tasting, getting reacquainted after a whole day apart.

His hands started roaming down my body, which reminded me of his gift.

"Wait."

"What's up?"

I sat up and took his hands, pressing them against my chest.

He gasped. "Micah."

I smiled as he read the message knitted on my sweater.

"I love you, Santi," he said aloud. "How? How did you do it?"

"My mom. I wasn't sure it was possible, but she saw it as a challenge. This can be our own secret code," I said.

"Also, an excuse for me to feel you up."

"That too."

"Please tell me there will be more."

I laughed. "She's working on it."

Santi pulled me into his arms and sucked the skin on the side of my neck. "How about we lower the oven and go make out naked in the bedroom?"

"Please."

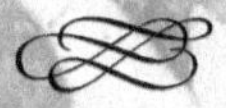

The rustling sound jolted me awake. There was something heavy on top of me, but my brain refused to cooperate, still tired from the weekend.

"Shh, go back to sleep."

"What?" I groaned. "What's going on?"

"Nothing, Sprinkles. You sleep now."

I opened my eyes to find Tom straddling me. "Baby, what are you doing? I mean, don't get me wrong, I'm usually up for some middle-of-the-night fun, but we just got back from Vegas and we're both working in the morning."

"I told you, go back to sleep," he said.

I sighed. "What's all this? Why is there fabric everywhere? And what's the time?"

"I'm doing your colors again because I think I'm going to make some changes to your wedding suit. And it's three."

I rubbed my eyes again and looked down. I had at least six different pieces of fabric on top of me. All different colors. And there was a measuring tape and a pair of scissors too.

"Angel, from where I'm lying, it looks like you're either plotting my murder or my funeral."

His slightly demonic laughter sent a shiver down my spine. I put the scissors and the measuring tape on the floor by the bed and threw the fabric on top, just in case.

"Baby," I said, pulling him down to lie on my chest. "What's going on in that gorgeous mind of yours?"

"I don't know. I'm scared."

"Of what?"

"All the things that could go wrong?"

I ran my hands down his back, trying to soothe him. "What do you think will go wrong?"

"What if Charlie doesn't make it to the wedding?"

"He'll be here."

He let out a frustrated sigh. "You don't know that. Where has he been all this time? He couldn't come to the bachelor weekend. He's barely calling these days. It's like he's hiding something. What if he's sick?" Tom gasped. "Oh my god, he's dying."

"Angel, listen to yourself. Do you really think that's true? That you wouldn't know by now if there was something wrong?"

"I don't know," he said in a high pitch. "When we went away for the weekend, Coco wasn't pregnant, and now she is. We didn't know, and now we do."

So that's what this was about.

"Angel, sometimes things happen, and we can't always control them. You've been working too hard on the wedding. I get that Coco's news has come as a surprise, but it'll be fine. If she has a full litter, I'm sure we'll find friends to adopt them. If not, we'll keep them all."

"Why are you so calm about this?" he asked.

"Because I'm meant to be your safe harbor in a storm, your rainbow after the rain."

He sighed. "I love you so much, Sprinkles."

"I love you too, Angel."

"Hey, wanna get up and bake cupcakes?"

I chuckled. "No, but I want to suck your dick until you fall asleep."

"Hmm, I think I can live with that." He jumped off me and laid on his back on his side of the bed, his cock already hard and ready to play.

"What am I going to do with you?"

"Suck my dick? You promised. Unless you still want to bake cupcakes."

I laughed.

"Life with you will never be boring, that's for sure."

"Thank you. Now suck." He pointed at his flushed cock.

Tom was beautiful in all colors, but when he was naked and ready for me, he was even more striking. I ran my hand over his body, paying attention to his nipples, kissing his stomach, belly button, and the tiny trail of hair that led to his cock.

"Wren," he begged.

"Do you want to bake cupcakes now?" I teased.

"Fuck no."

I raised my hand to his mouth. "Make it nice and wet for me, baby."

"Hmm..."

His desperation to be touched was clear when he opened his legs wide, exposing his hole. We were so compatible in bed it was unreal. Tom lived to be touched, and I lived to touch him.

I pressed my wet finger against his hole at the same time that I sucked his cock all the way down to the root.

He almost jumped off the bed. I moaned when he put his hands on my head and grabbed my hair. He wasn't pulling it hard, but it was enough that my dick was enjoying it.

I'd started with the intention of getting him off so he'd relax and sleep the rest of the night, but now I was all wired up.

"Baby, can I be inside you?" I asked.

"You never need to ask, Sprinkles."

I grabbed the bottle of lube and applied a generous amount to my cock and some to his hole.

"This is going to be over fast, baby."

"Give it to me, Wren."

I positioned myself on top of him and pulled his legs to rest over my shoulders. This always worked for Tom because it allowed me to go deeper and brush up against his prostate with every thrust.

"Yes! Fuck," he screamed as I bottomed out inside him.

"Say when, baby—"

"When!"

I pulled almost all the way out and then thrust back in again, first slowly and then picking up the pace until I was ramming my cock into Tom's tight hole.

"I'm not gonna last much longer," I said between gritted teeth.

"I'm there with you. Just a little...argh, fuck." His orgasm triggered mine as I fucked him into the mattress, powerless to stop.

I released his legs and lowered them down slowly. Even before I pulled out, Tom wrapped his arms around me and sought my mouth for a kiss.

"Thank you, baby. I really needed that," he said, sounding immediately sleepy.

I went to the bathroom, cleaned myself, and got a wet cloth to clean him. He snored softly through it all.

Coco walked back into the room and curled up on the bed on the other side of Tom.

"We'll need to have a little chat tomorrow, young lady," I said to her, stroking her head.

I settled against Tom, ready to sleep a few more hours.

My phone dinged just as I was drifting off. I picked it up to put it on silent when I saw it was a message from Coach Dempsey.

Have you thought about my offer yet? You're playing hard to get, but I have an increasing budget. If more money is what you need, we can work on that. Let me know.

SERGEI

Traveling by private jet was usually convenient unless it meant you couldn't use your flight as an excuse to attend a certain charity football game.

That and the fact that traveling overnight meant I'd sleep on the plane and arrive in Lydovia in the morning ready to go to work.

I'd even called Ryan and Zeke to check in on work, and they were both on top of things. Efficient bastards.

The game was at the high school football field. I parked the rental and looked around.

Why was the first thought that came to mind one of a young Rory coming to school with Connor? Probably feeling a little unsure but playing the part of a confident football player.

"Stop it now, Sergei. Rory is free now. He can test the waters, date someone in public, spend more time with his friends. Whatever happened in Vegas was good, but it stays in Vegas. The saying is there for a reason," I said aloud as if it made me listen to my own words better.

I got out of the car and followed the crowds gathering by the field.

There was a booth decorated with fairy lights a few yards away with a long line going to it. I recognized Tom straight away because he had a team jacket on, which was yellow and purple.

He was busy selling cakes and cookies. Right next to him was Indy serving hot drinks. I'd never been to an American football game, but this felt like the real deal, even though it was only a game between amateur teams to raise money for charity.

"Hey, Sergei." I looked around to follow the voice and saw James waving me to come over.

"Wren is squaring things off with the Stillwater team coach. The locker room is inside that building over there, and there are uniforms of different sizes, so pick whatever fits."

I laughed. "Sounds like this is taken very seriously."

"The food, hot drinks, cheering, and after-party? Absolutely. The actual playing? Not so much. Most of these guys have full-time jobs and aren't quite at the peak of their fitness."

"Speak for yourself," Slade said.

I tapped his arm. "I thought you were part of the resistance."

"So did I, but it seems these days I'm all about branching out into new horizons or some shit like that," he said.

"I'll go get changed then."

On my way over to the building, I spotted Rory. He

was talking to Connor and some other guy. Both were in the team uniform.

I was going to need all my strength to stop myself from pulling Rory aside and having my way with him. Especially when he was wearing shorts that were an ode to his perfect butt.

No, it was no good going there because he'd made it clear what he wanted.

I found the changing room easily and was relieved to find a uniform that fit my larger frame. I changed and ran back out to join the team.

Everybody was gathered around. I couldn't why because they were in a circle, but as I got closer, it made sense.

"Look here. You can get black eyes, scratches, stains, ouchies, and boo-boos. Get all your boy shit out of your system. But under no circumstances are you to break any limbs. Got it?" Tom shouted loud enough for everyone to hear.

"Got it!" the team shouted back.

He made eye contact with me as he returned to the booth. "Someone has to keep the guys in check," he said.

I laughed. "Don't ever change, Tom."

"I don't intend to," he said. "Now go kick ass and help my man win the game."

I was probably not the best person to put that responsibility on. First of all, I hadn't trained with the team. Wren sent us a message with our positions, but it wasn't until just before the game that he showed us the playbook.

Second of all, the number of times I'd actually played

the game was limited since it wasn't a popular sport in Lydovia.

"Okay, guys, gather round. You heard Tom. Bring all your limbs home, and you get free brownies. Get a trip to the hospital, and you're eating bad Jell-O. Your choice. Remember, this is a friendly game. We want to entertain the crowds. Having said that, please do kick ass. We won last year, so we have a reputation to uphold. It also means Stillwater will be doing their best to throw us off the throne and into the dungeon."

The guys all cheered and then gathered closer while Wren ran through the playbook. I followed the best I could.

The first half of the game wasn't too bad, but I noticed some of the players on the opposite team kept going for Rory. I could tell what they were trying to do.

Intimidation and elimination. Both teams had limited players, so even with unlimited swaps, it paid off if a player was nervous on the field.

We all gathered around Wren at the halftime break.

"Wren, what the hell are they doing. They keep going for Rory. What's that all about?" I asked.

"I saw that. I'll have a word with their coach. We don't play dirty here." He turned to Rory. "How are you holding up?"

"Fine. I can look after myself," he said while staring straight into my eyes.

"Okay. I gotta say, you've lost none of your speed since high school. The only way you'll not be part of this team now is if you move to another country," Wren said.

Now that was an idea. Lydovia was a perfectly safe

country with a low crime rate and no stupid weird contact sports.

The second half went straight into dirty plays by the other team. Wren warned the coach, but he didn't seem to care.

Even a couple of the players came over to apologize, saying the coach was new and this wasn't how they usually did things.

The words were appreciated, but unless they were followed by actions, they didn't mean anything.

My fitness was definitely pushed to the limit as I ran along the field blocking the other team's plays.

I'd just thrown the ball over to James, who had a clean shot at scoring, when two guys came from my left side and hit me with full force.

Everything went dark for a moment, and I stopped hearing the crowd.

Warm hands touched my neck and my face.

"Sergei."

My vision came back slowly, and I found myself staring into Rory's worried eyes. "Hey," I said.

"Hey."

"How do you feel?" he asked.

"Like I was hit by a truck."

He kept staring at me and then looking up. I couldn't take my eyes off him.

"Kitten," I said.

He looked down at me and then up again. "He's fine," he said and then stood up.

The exchange must have lasted only a few seconds, but it felt like a lot longer. Wren rushed over and helped me up.

"I'm stopping the game and reporting the other team. Come on. Let's eat some brownies."

"I should probably head to the airport," I said.

Was I running?

Absolutely.

Did it hurt?

Like a motherfucker.

I looked for Sergei all over the palace and couldn't find him. I even resorted to calling his mom, and she hadn't heard from him since he'd returned from Chester Falls days ago.

What the hell had happened out there?

There was only one other person who could always find Sergei. The only problem was that he'd been holed up in the office with his sister all afternoon with the transportation minister.

Alexi was still at school, so I waited in the bedroom, sitting in the middle of the bed with my sketchpad drawing until Kris came into our room.

"Hey, gorgeous," he said in that voice that always made me swoon.

"Hey, have you seen Sergei?"

Kris pouted. "Should I be worried that after being apart from you for"—he looked at his watch—"six hours, the first thing you ask is where's my ex?"

I rolled my eyes and got off the bed. "I want to speak to him, but I can't find him anywhere."

"His thinking place is the glasshouse on the far side of the pond," Kris said and gave me a kiss that warmed me up enough to withstand the cold temperatures outside. "Wrap up warm, baby."

I grabbed my heavy winter coat and went out looking for Sergei. As Kris had predicted, I found Sergei inside the glasshouse. He was staring at the flowers growing from an old fountain.

"Hey," I said.

He looked up and smiled. "Any news?"

"Yeah, we sign the adoption papers tomorrow. Alexi has officially moved in. We're announcing to my family in two days and to the press the day after that."

Sergei nodded. "Congratulations. I'm really happy for you and Kris. Alexi is a great kid."

I smiled, thinking about my son. God, I was a father now. And to a teenager, nonetheless. "He's amazing. But what I want to know is about you."

I sat next to him, thankful my coat was long enough that I didn't have to sit on the freezing stone bench.

"What about me?"

"Tell me about Chester Falls. How was the bachelor party?"

He kept staring straight ahead at the flowers. "It was really good. Everyone enjoyed it. Good choice of club, by the way. Half of us never made it there, but Tom and some of the guys came back really buzzed and happy."

"That's good."

"Dancing class didn't go too well though."

He ran through the incidents with the class and the strippers, and I lost it. I laughed so hard I thought I was going to cry. I was so gutted that I couldn't be there for Tom and Wren. I just hoped they understood my reason when I told them about Alexi.

"Anything else?" I asked.

He shrugged. "There was a football game yesterday to raise money for a charity founded by a local vet. The game was stopped because of foul play."

"Oh no, did a chicken run through the field again? That used to happen all the time until they put the fences up."

He looked at me. "Huh?"

"Fowl play. Sorry, I couldn't resist." I bumped his arm.

"Oh my god, you're already doing bad dad jokes. I hope you understand it's downhill from this moment on," he said.

I laughed. "If you all had a great time, then why are you so broody? What happened?"

"Nothing happened."

I gave him my most threatening look, which, when you were my size and had bright-red hair, was never very menacing.

"Must have been something if you're here instead of the gym, your office, or with Kris."

Sergei let out a breath.

"He was right," he said.

"Who?"

"Kris."

I laughed. "He's been known to be once or twice. What was he right about this time?"

"Rory."

I stiffened. "What do you mean?"

"He said Rory has many layers and that he might surprise me."

"And did he?"

Sergei smiled. "If you told me I was swapped at birth with Kris and I'm the actual Prince of Lydovia, I'd be less surprised."

"Rory...he's...I don't know what to say," I said.

"I know." Sergei put his hand on mine. "He told me what happened between you."

"He still hasn't forgiven himself. I mean, it's taken me a long time to get over it, but I can see he's changed. To be honest, knowing him now, I wonder if what I thought happened was real or fabricated by him to push me away for my protection."

Sergei squeezed my hand before letting go.

"He's...I don't know. He has this prickly exterior. He's like a kitten who'll try to growl and hiss at you even when you're bringing him food. But when you look him in the eye, you see all he wants is a warm and cozy place to sleep and tummy rubs."

It was all making sense now, but I needed to tread carefully because I knew Sergei would bolt if things got too personal for him.

"Sergei, do you want to talk about it? After all, I have some experience with Rory."

He stood and walked around the bench, looking at the garden.

"He let me in. He told me things he'd never told anyone. He got me and didn't judge me for what happened with Kris when we broke up. He made me laugh, and he made me...fuck...I can't do this." He walked to the door of the greenhouse, but I was quick enough to grab his sleeve to stop him.

"Sergei, did you...do you have feelings for Rory?"

He didn't say anything for the longest time. When he did, it was barely audible.

"Yes."

"Tom told me he came out to the group. Based on what you just said, I'm going to take a wild guess that he also has feelings for you."

"Maybe he does, but he's just come out. He's figuring himself out, and I'm not looking for something temporary. Besides, he wanted to keep it a secret. I've been there and don't wish to return."

Sergei had a valid point. I'd heard all the stories from Kris. The press hadn't been particularly kind to Sergei.

"Honey, things may have changed for Rory, but he's still the same guy who's been in the shadow of his parents his whole life. The same guy who learned what family is from someone else's family. He may need to hear he's a good person more than a few times until he believes it."

He seemed to think about what I said for a moment.

"Do you think he pushed me away to protect me from himself?"

"I don't know, and neither will you until you ask. You don't have to have everything figured out straight away, especially as you just connected, but talking and being honest is a good start."

Sergei nodded. "Thank you, Charlie."

I hugged him tightly. Chuckling when he tensed a little before giving up trying to resist my embrace. He'd always been a little shy around me, which I suspected was because of Kris. He didn't want to be the cause of any issues between us.

"You're a good man, Sergei. I hope you know that I love you very much, and so does Kris."

"Right back at you." He kissed my hair and then pulled away.

We walked back inside together. Kris was with Alexi in the piano room.

Kris was playing, and Alexi was drawing on his sketchpad.

"Hey, sweetie, how was school?" I asked.

"It was fine."

Alexi was usually chatty when it came to talking about his day. After being denied a proper education for years, he was thriving in the class environment, and even after only a few months, he'd managed to almost catch up with the rest of the class.

"What's bothering you? Is there anything you need in your room? Do you want to invite a friend over?"

He shook his head. "No...I...um...would you tell me more about your family? I've never had grandparents or uncles before. I'm a little nervous about meeting them all at your friend's wedding."

Kris must have heard Alexi because he stopped playing and came to sit with us.

"Well, Sergei and your father have had some experience with my family, so they can tell you all about it."

Sergei snorted. "My advice is limited, kid, but this is what I learned. Your family has really weird pets. You might want to avoid your Aunt Gina, but smile for your grand-mother, and you'll have a friend for life. Don't learn how to cook from your granddad, and make sure to go to Benny's on a Sunday morning because they always give you an extra pancake with your stack."

I shook my head. "I guess that's all very practical and also accurate advice. Kris?"

He seemed to think about it for a moment before he spoke. "Your dad's family accepted me as one of them when all they knew about me was that I was Charlie's boyfriend. When my identity was revealed, instead of pushing me away, they all got even closer, like a protective chain. I hope Chester Falls will feel like a home to you as it does to me."

Alexi nodded and then looked at me.

"Sergei and your father are both right. You will receive unconditional love. But it'll be crazy love. I'll help you remember who's who before the wedding, okay?"

"Okay, thanks, Dad."

"My pleasure. Now we should all get ready for dinner. Mimi is doing her special macaroni and cheese," I said.

"That's my favorite." Alexi beamed and stood up straight away. "I'll go get ready."

I watched him as he left the room and then turned to Kris, holding his hand. "He's perfect, isn't he?"

"He's perfect for us," Kris said.

"Ugh, you guys are so disgustingly in love. I'm going to wash up before dinner."

When Sergei left, I straddled Kris's lap and kissed him.

Sergei was right. We were disgustingly in love, and I wouldn't change it for anything in the world. I just hoped we were a good influence on him, and he plucked up the courage to speak to Rory. Truly speak to Rory.

RORY

Was it me, or was this winter colder than usual?

Okay, so I'd spent the last couple of winters in Singapore, where the weather was considerably milder, but this felt like blizzard weather.

The doorbell rang just as I put on a warmer sweater than the one I'd been wearing. I ran downstairs in my socks. There was a chance I'd end up with a broken neck from slipping on the wooden floor, but I was determined to catch the mail carrier. It had been twice now that I'd been home and somehow still missed a parcel delivery.

"Coming!"

I opened the door, but instead of the mail carrier, I found myself staring at Sergei, who looked like a snow prince in his expensive coat, bright-blue eyes, and knit cap.

He smiled. "Hi."

"Hi."

"Can I come in?"

I wanted to say no, but my feet moved of their own accord.

He closed the door behind himself but didn't move beyond.

"Um...what are you doing here?" I asked.

"That's a question that has many potential answers, and I'm not sure where to start. Can I take you somewhere?"

I stared at him.

"Please?"

"Okay." I grabbed my coat from the hanger by the door.

"Rory?"

"What?"

"As adorable as you look in your teddy bear pajamas, it might be a good idea to change into something warmer."

I looked down and let out a sigh. "Oh...give me a few minutes."

I went back upstairs to change into my jeans and put on a warmer pair of socks. The sweater would have to do because it was the warmest one I had.

Sergei had a different car this time, and when I got inside, I realized why. It was warm and cozy and probably better in the snow than the car he'd had before.

"Where are we going?" I asked.

"Have you ever had lavender honey?"

"No, can't say I have."

He smiled. "Neither have I, but I'm assured it's the best thing since sliced bread, which by the way, is an expression I never understood."

I stared at him as he drove us out of Chester Falls through the country roads. For a moment, I thought he was taking us to Stillwater, but then he took a different turn.

The longer Sergei stayed silent in the car, the more I wanted to shout. What the hell were we doing? Where were we going? And why was he in Chester Falls a whole week before Tom and Wren's wedding?

"Are Charlie and Kris in Chester Falls?" I asked, breaking the silence.

"No, they're waiting for Alexi's passport to arrive, so it's likely to be a couple of days before the wedding."

I still couldn't believe Charlie and Kris had adopted a teenage kid.

Shortly after the bachelor weekend, they'd requested that everyone close to them gather at Charlie's parents' house. I'd thought they were revealing some kind of wedding gift for the grooms, but they were announcing their adoption news over a video call.

I remembered hoping for a glimpse of Sergei in the call, especially since his mom, Mimi, who was a family friend, was also there to greet everyone.

Mimi sounded like such a great woman and the best mom to have. The way she talked about Kris and Charlie was as if they were her own sons. It made me sad for having such a dysfunctional upbringing, but also lucky to have still experienced some healthy parenting from Connor's parents.

"We're here," Sergei said.

"Where's here?" I'd been so lost in my thoughts, I hadn't even noticed when we'd left the main road.

"This is Reed's farm. I booked us a honey-tasting experience, but first, I want to show you something."

"A honey-tasting experience?" I must have been dreaming because there was no way one moment I was at home alone in my PJs and the next I was going to taste honey. I mean, honey is honey, right?

"Reed has the best monofloral honey. The bees pollinate his lavender fields and collect the nectar so the honey smells and tastes of lavender. He's recently started offering different kinds of experiences at the farm during the winter instead of closing for customers."

I followed Sergei around a large circular building. There were a few people around, mostly going inside the building.

We walked through a small path that led to a brick wall with an iron gate. Sergei opened the gate, and we walked through.

On the other side were rows upon rows of fluffy white snow, following the shape of the land as far as I could see. I suspected there were rows of lavender under the snow because in the distance, right in the middle of the field, there was an area that didn't have any snow and I could see the lavender.

"What's that?" I asked.

"Apparently, bees generate heat to keep warm in the winter, and there are so many hives that it raises the temperature in that part of the field...or something like that. Reed explained it to me over the phone, but I couldn't take it all in. He's a little excitable when he talks about honey."

"Okay, that makes sense." What didn't make sense was why we were here.

Sergei waited for a couple to walk past us, and then he took my hands in his.

"Rory, I have something to tell you, and I need you to listen until the end, okay? Then if you want, I can take you home."

"Okay."

He seemed to steel himself, and he looked into my eyes as he spoke.

"Rory, I've been doing a lot of thinking recently. That, and I've had a lecture or three from Charlie and Kris, but we won't go there."

He smiled when he mentioned Charlie and Kris but then went serious again. My heart rate increased, and despite the cold, I felt the skin around my neck warm.

"I have to apologize for my behavior," he said. "When you asked if we could keep things between us, I went into a place in the past when I wasn't happy. When I had to keep my feelings from everyone, including my mom. That was the hardest thing I've ever done in my life because there's only the two of us, and we're really close. But I understood it was harder for Kris to come out, so we pretended to be friends while we were so much more. Then when we were forced to come out, the press shredded me to pieces. It took me a while to recover from that. Maybe in some ways, I never did, which was why I ended up in the press again when we broke up."

"I'm sorry," I said.

He took a small tentative step toward me and brought my hands up to his chest, linking our gloved fingers.

"Anyway, that's why I pulled away from you. I made assumptions about what you wanted based on my own insecurities, and then I behaved like an asshole. But I never told you what I wanted. I never gave you the option to decide for yourself."

I swallowed dry. "What...do you want?"

"You, Rory. I want you on such a deep level that it

makes me wonder if I've ever really understood what love was or if I was tricked by my inexperience. I want to date you, to live with you, and to build a life together. I want to learn how to cook because you'll complain that I was far too spoiled growing up in a palace. I'm not sure I want kids, but I'd be open to discussion if you want them. And most of all, I want you to want all of that too, with me."

"Why?" Out of all the things I could have said to follow his heartwarming speech, I had to go and be a dick.

And this was why I was going to be alone forever.

He released my hands but pressed them against his chest so I wouldn't remove them, and then he took his gloves off and touched my face.

I closed my eyes and took a deep breath, enjoying the warm, soft touch.

"Because, Rory, you're everything. We are the same, but we're also not. When you're upset, you bring out your claws. When I'm upset, I brood. But we've both been misguided. We've both struggled with ourselves. According to Charlie, we both need to do some inner forgiving. I'm willing to work on that if it means I get to keep you. I know I can be the man you need, and I know you are everything I want. So all I'm asking is, Rory, do you want to take a chance on us? Come to the wedding with me. As your date, as your boyfriend, whatever you want to call it as long as I get to be yours."

Sergei became a blurry figure in front of me as my eyes filled with tears.

"Please don't cry, baby," he said with such a gentle voice that I couldn't help the sob that came out of me.

He held me tight. Wrapping his arms around me like a force field.

"I'm sorry. I...I've been keeping it together for such a long time that this was bound to happen." I cleared the tears and looked back at him. "I didn't want to keep you a secret, Sergei. You have to know that. I just needed to figure out what was happening because it felt too big, too important, and too good. I didn't believe it. I thought maybe you just wanted to comfort me. And I didn't trust myself to not hurt you."

"What are you saying, Kitten?"

His use of the nickname he gave me made me smile.

"I'm saying that I'm right there with you. I want all those things...with you."

"Oh, Kitten," he breathed out before he pressed his lips against mine.

Our breaths steamed up in the cold. My nose was frozen, and I was pretty sure my hair might break in this temperature because I'd forgotten to bring a hat. But Sergei's lips were warm. His tongue was delicious, and as we kissed for the longest time, other parts of my body warmed up too.

We held each other for a while after our lips parted.

"Why did you pick this place? You know you could have done this in my living room by the fire, right?" I said.

Sergei laughed. "It would have definitely made it easier to get naked, so I'm now seeing the flaw in my plan. I picked this place because I wanted you to see the snow and ask for a clean slate. Under that snow, there are still rows upon rows of lavender bushes, and come spring, they'll be ready to flower, just like us."

"I never took you for a hopeless romantic," I teased even as my stomach fluttered with millions of butterflies.

"I might need to see a doctor. I'm also concerned about this."

We laughed, and he held my hand as he walked to a building where we were met by a guy holding a toddler.

"Hi there, can I help?" he asked.

"We're booked for the honey experience," Sergei said.

The guy looked at the computer for a while and then started typing one-handed. "Ah, yeah, gotcha. Sorry about this. This is bring-your-kid-to-work day, also known as it's-snowed-so-the-world-is-taking-a-break day."

I smiled at the kid, and he waved at me. How cute.

"I'm Callan, by the way. I'm the farm manager. Reed isn't here today, but I assure you you'll be well looked after."

Callan took us to a table by a window where we had a perfect view of the white fields.

Sergei took my hand and held it on the table. "I can't believe it was this easy. Kris and Charlie are going to be so smug."

I laughed. "I guess they were right. It's not hard when it's meant to be. But we don't need to tell them that."

It was his turn to laugh, and I could already see the cogs turning in his head.

"How are Tom and Wren getting on with the wedding prep? I'll be around all week, and I suppose I can't keep you in bed for the duration so I could help out in my spare time."

"You are making many assumptions there."

"Only one. That you're mine and I'm not letting you go."

Heart suitably melted.

"I'll see what I can do. Do you want to stay at my place?" I asked.

"Kitten, I was counting on it. My bags are in the trunk of the car."

I laughed and shook my head, but then I remembered his question.

"I'm actually a little worried about Tom. I haven't seen him stand still in the last few weeks. The wedding stuff is all done, but there's something unsettling him."

"Like what?"

"I wish I knew. He was so excited about Charlie's news and being a godparent to Alexi that he started making notes for a party to welcome him formally in the spring. But I don't think that's it. I'm just a little worried he'll run himself into the ground and won't enjoy his big day."

"We can stop by his place on the way to yours if you want," Sergei said. I smiled at him, feeling all kinds of warm and fuzzy feelings that made me want to be home and naked with him.

"That would be great."

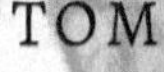

"*A* girl should be two things: classy and fabulous," I said to the mannequin I was dressing by the window. "Remember Coco's words because they are wise. She didn't do fashion. She *was* fashion."

I looked at the pencil portrait of my muse and smiled. She was my constant companion and source of inspiration. Charlie's amazing drawing had hung on the wall at Fabulize since the day I opened the doors, and it was still my signature wall.

It was almost two years since I'd opened my store, and sometimes I still didn't believe I was living my dream.

Every day opened a new potential to make someone's day a little more special. I couldn't imagine myself doing anything else.

I looked out the window and thought I recognized the man standing on the other side of the road. He looked at me, and after a moment, he started crossing the street toward Fabulize.

"Good morning, welcome to Fabulize. Pardon my memory, but I've met you before, haven't I?" I asked.

The guy stretched his hand out. "Riley Dempsey."

"Oh, yes, of course. You used to be Wren's coach. Nice to see you again. Are you looking for a new outfit? Maybe a special occasion coming up?"

He smiled and said, "Tom, could we have a talk?"

"Of course, come over to the couch. Can I get you something to drink?"

"No, thank you."

"Okay."

I sat on the edge of the couch, and the coach sat next to me.

"I'm going to be upfront with you, Tom. Wren has the opportunity to play in the big league again, and I'm afraid he's going to pass it up."

"What do you mean?" Wren couldn't play anymore since the surgery. Even though his knee seemed to be stronger since the last surgery, he hadn't given any indication he was fit enough.

"Wren was a good player, but he wasn't great. What he was great at was coaching others. He did it all the time. He'd memorize the plays and help the team."

"He never talks much about his playing days. I think he misses it, but he loves being a coach."

He nodded. "That's why I'm talking to you. Maybe you can help him make the right decision. I'm looking for an assistant coach, and I know Wren is the right person for the job. He's settling in here, and he deserves more. He has the talent to do more."

I couldn't say I disagreed with the coach, but what did that mean? Would we need to move?

"What exactly are your terms, Coach? Wren loves being close to his family, especially since his dad had a heart attack. He has his friends here, and he loves his job."

He pulled a folded piece of paper from the inside pocket of his coat and gave it to me.

"What's this?"

"This is a copy of the offer I made Wren...but with a few updates."

I read through and gasped when I saw the original figure with a line through it and a new amount written above it that was almost twice as much. Not just that, the team was offering to foot the full moving expense and set us up with an apartment until we found our own place.

The coach was looking at me full of expectation when I looked up.

"You're a businessman, Tom. You know that's a damn good offer."

"I...I don't know what to say. This needs to be Wren's decision."

"He's been sitting on this for over a month. My gut feeling is that what's stopping him is you. He's putting you first. Closing your shop and opening in San Diego isn't a guarantee of success, so you'd be taking a big risk. The figure you see accounts for that risk."

I was in too much shock to process everything he was saying.

Was I holding Wren back? But how was I when I didn't even know there was a possibility he might be offered a job in San Diego?

"Mr. Dempsey, I'm not comfortable in this position. This needs to be something Wren and I discuss together. The fact you're cornering me without Wren knowing about it, I assume, says something about the kind of people he'd be working with if he accepted your offer. I'd like you to leave now, please."

He didn't say a word as he left the store. I was still shaking and rooted to my spot minutes later.

Why hadn't Wren told me about this? Did it mean he didn't want to go? Or maybe he did, but he didn't know how to approach it.

Only a few days ago, I was talking about hiring someone to help me with the store so I could take on more styling jobs. That part of the business was booming, but I didn't always have time for it.

I thought about it some more and formed a plan in my head.

First stop, Spilled Beans.

I closed the store and walked over to the coffee shop. Bubble was his usual cheery self, but he must have noticed *I* wasn't my usual self because he said Indy was at the back and didn't say anything else.

"Oh hey, groom-to-be, how are you?" Indy said, placing two baking tins with batter in the oven.

"I need to ask you a question."

"Sure."

"I don't know how to word this...when you and Tate made up and decided to be together, did you always know he'd move to Chester Falls?"

Indy grabbed a cloth and started cleaning his workbench.

"Yes but no. We talked about it. Me moving to Boston was the least likely outcome because I wouldn't have been able to keep my business open. Tate was already unhappy with his job and considering opening his own practice, so it made sense for him to move to Chester Falls. And Tristan was here too, which was a big part of it."

"What if he'd been really happy with his job? Would you have moved?"

Indy looked like he was considering it.

"I don't think I'd do it straight away. Tate and I are partners, which means we're both equally important. Spilled Beans is my career and dream. I mean, this is pie in the sky thinking, but maybe I'd have given it a year to sell the business here and see if it was possible to open my own coffee shop in Boston. I don't know. Long-distance relationships are hard, but we'd make it work."

"Okay..."

"What is this about? Are you thinking of moving? I thought you were happy here," he said.

I sighed. "I am...we are...it's just...it's probably nothing."

Indy gave me an understanding look. "I'm here if you want to talk. Anytime, okay?"

I went around the workbench and gave him a hug. "Thanks, babe. I know I can."

He put his hands on my shoulders. "Promise me one thing." I nodded. "Whatever's happening, you're not going to run from Wren or the situation. You're going to talk it out."

"I Coco promise."

He smiled, knowing I really meant it if I called out my muse.

"Thank you for listening. I've gotta do something, so I'm closing early. I'll see you tomorrow, okay?"

"Okay, honey. If you come in early, you might get to see your wedding cake baking in progress."

"Oh my gosh, I'll be here with bells on. I'd say I'll bring cake but..." I gestured around.

He laughed. "Off you go then."

"See ya."

When I went back into the front, Bubble was sticking googly eyes onto the cold beverages.

"What are you doing?"

"Oh my sweet Jesus, I'm gonna need a paramedic," he said, placing his hands on his chest.

"You'll be fine."

"No, seriously. You can't walk up on people like that."

I gave him a look.

"Fine, I'm adding googly eyes to the drinks because I think they look more friendly that way."

"Why do drinks need to be friendly? You know what? Don't answer that. Can you make me a rainbow unicorn latte with cream and sprinkles to go, please?"

He put his hands on his hips. "You know that's not on the menu, darling."

"It is for me." I gave him my sparkliest smile, and he returned it, going behind the counter to prepare my drink.

For all his attitude, Bubble was an adorable marsh-mallow and I know I'd miss him as much as I would all of my older friends.

Not that I was leaving...at least I hoped I wasn't...ugh, I didn't know anymore.

"Thanks, sweetie," I said, paying for my drink.

My first stop was home to grab some stuff I needed and leave immediately.

WREN

"Honey, I'm home," I said as I got in.

There was no reply, which was strange because he was usually home before me. I went into the garage, and his car wasn't there. Another odd thing.

Tom always walked to work, and he hadn't mentioned anything about having any appointments after the store closed.

We'd decided to have the rest of last night's chicken for dinner, so I went up to the bedroom to grab a shower.

Tom had been a little stressed with the wedding, making lists, crossing things off. I was sure his lists had lists.

I could light some candles, open a bottle of wine, and make him chill with me. And if he didn't want to, I'd use one of my many tricks.

When I opened the bedroom door, I saw his coat on the bed.

Where would he go without his coat?

I picked it up to hang it in the wardrobe when a piece of paper fell on the carpet.

As soon as I saw it, I recognized it immediately.

What the fuck?

My heart sank at the thought that Tom found the offer from the Marinos and came to the wrong conclusion, but then I saw this one had a small but quite significant update.

What the hell is going on?

Why did Tom have a copy of my offer with a larger sum written on it?

I picked up my phone and called Coach Dempsey.

"Hello?"

"Coach, it's Wren. I'm not going to apologize for going straight to the point. What right did you think you had approaching my fiancé to discuss the offer you made?"

"Wren, it's been a month, and the bosses want an answer. There's only so long they're willing to wait. Hence the updated incentive."

My blood felt like it was boiling.

"With all due respect, your boss is your problem, not mine. I don't appreciate you going behind my back to influence my decision. What did you do? Convince Tom that we would be financially better off in San Diego? That he'd be selfish not to support me and this opportunity?"

"Well, I...I didn't put it that way."

I let out a laugh. "Of course you didn't, but I bet your message was received loud and clear."

"Wren, if you know about the offer, does this mean that—"

"It means that you've made my evening a lot more exciting but not in a good way. Please don't contact me again. I'm not interested in taking the job in San Diego. As much as I was considering it, you've shown me exactly what kind of people I'd be working with, so no, thanks."

"Son, you know how this goes. It's business."

I laughed. "Doesn't mean I have to like or accept it."

I hung up and dialed Tom's number.

The phone rang until it went to voicemail.

"Hey, baby. Please call me back. I know you know about San Diego. We need to talk about it, okay? Please call me or come home. Please..."

My heart felt tight at the thought that Tom might be out there wondering if I was going to take a job three thousand miles away.

"Gina!"

I searched for Charlie's aunt's number. She and Tom were close, so there was a chance he might go there.

"Hello, Wren, darling," she said.

"Hi, Gina. Is Tom with you?"

"No, sweetie. Why?"

"No reason. Thank you. Speak soon."

"All right, honey. Be good."

I smiled. Charlie's aunt was a little crazy, but she was a sweetheart.

Okay, so he wasn't with Gina. Maybe Indy?

Instead of walking, I jumped back in the car and drove to Spilled Beans. They were about to close, but Bubble saw me and opened the door.

"Hey, Thor. Do you need help polishing your hammer?"

"Not now, Bubble. Is Indy here?"

"Sure, in the back. Is everything okay?" he asked, sounding really worried.

"To be honest, I don't know."

Indy didn't seem all that surprised to see me.

"Ugh, he's disappeared again, hasn't he?" he sighed.

I nodded. "What do you know?"

"He was here earlier asking questions about when Tate and I got together and how we decided where to live. What's going on?"

I ran my hands over my hair. "I got a job offer from the Marinos—one I don't have any intention to accept—but Tom doesn't know that. He just found out and probably thinks I want to accept."

"Oh, Tom," Indy said with a sigh. "I made him promise he wouldn't run. I didn't think he would."

"What do I do?"

"Is he answering his phone?"

I shook my head.

He came over and put his arms around me. "Don't panic. Keep trying to get through. You're about to get married. That won't change for all the jobs in the world. Maybe he just needs some space to think."

"Yeah, you're right. I'll go home and wait for him. He'll be back...right?"

"He will be."

I left Spilled Beans and made my way home.

As I turned the corner, I saw the light on inside straight away. I sped up like a quarterback running with the football, hoping to score a touchdown.

I had enough presence of mind to stop the car and put it in park before I got out and ran inside.

"Tom!"

"Office," he replied.

I found him still with his work suit on, so he hadn't been back long. He was in front of a large whiteboard we didn't have before.

"Oh my god, baby." I walked up to him and pulled him into my arms, claiming his mouth. He responded immediately, holding tight and reaching to every lick of my tongue on his.

"Wow, Sprinkles," he said, out of breath.

"Tom—" He put his hand up to stop me.

"Baby, we need to talk, but please let me talk first, okay?" he asked.

I nodded.

"So, I'm working on a plan, and I think we can make this work. If they're going to be sneaky, then we're going to play dirty too. These are my rules." He pointed to the bullet points on the whiteboard. "Number one, no one is going anywhere until after the honeymoon. Number two, we're picking a place together. Number three, we'll keep our house until we're sure we want to move permanently. Number four—"

I put my hand on his mouth.

"No."

"No?"

"No."

"You want a different plan? Okay, we can work on it. Let me erase this, and we can start over. I have extra pens and pink sticky notes."

I smiled. No wonder I fell in love with this man so quickly. He really was the most special person in the world.

"No, baby. We're not going anywhere," I said.

"We're not? But the offer."

I held his hands close to my chest. "I know Riley came to see you. He was misguided, and his impatience has quashed any feelings I had about the job."

"So you were considering it..."

"For a hot second. Angel, I love football, and I love coaching. More than I thought I would. It's been clear to me for a while that even if I hadn't had the injury, I'd probably still end up with a short playing career, taking up coaching."

"He said the same thing."

"He's a smart man. Wonderful coach. But he's wrong about one thing."

"What's that?"

"I prefer coaching the kids at school. With them, I have an opportunity to shape them not only as players but as people. My job goes beyond coaching the sport. They trust me and look up to me. Two weeks ago, one of the kids suggested we let girls join the team. Another one gave me a list of ideas for how the team can get involved with Pride month next year. Their grades are up, and they're engaged. *This* is how I'm going to make a difference in the world."

Tom let out a long sigh, all the tension he was holding in his tiny frame evaporating.

"I'm so happy to hear you say that. I didn't want to be the one to hold you back if this was what you really wanted. But I can see how much you love the kids and your job. Even if half the adult population in town crosses the road to the other side when they see you, out of fear you'll ask them to play sports."

I laughed. "I've gained a reputation, haven't I?"

"Just a little," he said, pinching his thumb and pointer finger together.

"I do love you for throwing yourself into this only days away from our wedding. You are totally insane and wonderful, and I couldn't be prouder to be your husband."

I kissed him again until he was moaning and asking for more.

Dinner was going to be very, very late because first I needed to get up and close with my future husband.

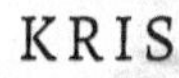

KRIS

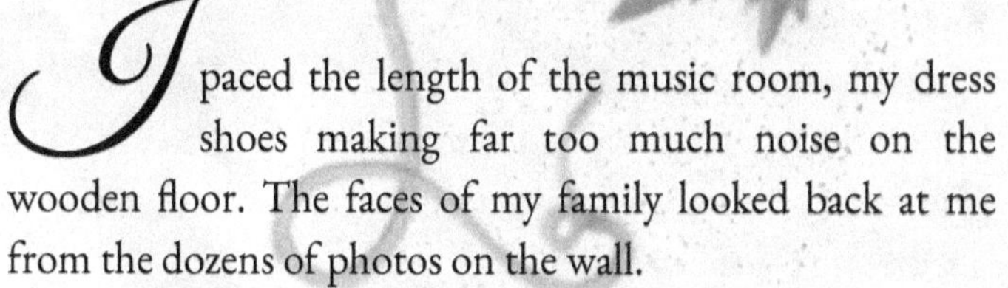

I paced the length of the music room, my dress shoes making far too much noise on the wooden floor. The faces of my family looked back at me from the dozens of photos on the wall.

Charlie and I on our wedding day. Everyone in the palace gardens the first time Charlie's family visited. Sergei and Mimi forcing Charlie to try spiced apple tea, Lydovia's specialty drink which he hated to start with but then developed a taste for.

More recently, there were photos of us at other family events, Charlie proudly opening his gallery and the most important one, us with our son, Alexi.

So much had changed in the last two years that if someone had asked me if I ever imagined this to be my life, I'd have said I was more likely to be the next man on the moon.

I turned around at the sound of footsteps and smiled at the sight of my husband walking toward me in a perfectly fitted suit, his red hair styled and his eyes as soulful as ever.

"What do you think?"

I held out my hand. He took it without question.

"You look beautiful, baby. If we weren't married already, I'd pop the question right now." I ran my nose up his neck and inhaled. "Hmm, you smell divine."

"I'm going to kick you in the balls if you make me get an erection while wearing this suit," he said.

"Jesus, guys, can you ever give it a rest?"

Charlie looked at me and smiled at Alexi's comment.

"Probably not, son. You'll have to get used to it," I said.

He rolled his eyes. "Ugh, the curse of having two dads that love each other."

He looked great in his suit.

He'd spent the night at Charlie's parents' place, so I was glad to see he'd managed to get up in time to come home to get dressed for the wedding.

Just as we'd hoped, Alexi had fit perfectly within Charlie's family, and especially his mom was loving spoiling him. After his challenging start in life, Alexi deserved all the spoiling. Although I was going to need to keep an eye on it before it got out of hand.

Charlie and I were determined to raise Alexi to have as much of a normal life as possible, despite his new royal title.

"Come on, you dashing princes, let me take you to the ball," Zeke said from the door. "Team 1 is ready, and team 2 is on standby for your arrival."

"Thanks, Zeke."

Tom had picked Connor and James's estate to host the venue not just for loyalty and friendship to Charlie's brother but also because it was a secure place for us. The press still liked to follow us around when we were in the States despite our mostly domestic activities.

How boring to take photos of a family attending a barbecue or meeting friends for coffee. But it was part of the deal of being a royal, so we managed it.

These days, thanks to Charlie, Lydovia's sweetheart, we mostly received good press, which made my sister's job a lot easier. She could focus on what really mattered as the reigning queen of Lydovia, and soon to be proud momma.

When we arrived at Lexington-Bennet Hall, everything seemed ready to go, so we were taken straight to the gardens, where the ceremony would take place by the pond.

"Wow, this place is really cool," Alexi said.

There were dozens of black Christmas trees decorated with silver ornaments and a rainbow star on top. Against the snowy white background, the trees really stood out.

"Hey guys," Connor said, coming over. "Just so you know, I'm not stressing about this at all. Go pick a seat, and I'll join you soon."

James walked past holding a radio. "Just so you know, he's really stressing."

I chuckled.

"I'll go check on Tom," Charlie said.

"Okay, see you later. Love you." I gave him a quick kiss and then took a seat with Alexi to wait for the start of the ceremony.

Wren and Aiden were already waiting by the arch, which was covered in pink, blue, and purple flowers. I thought it was a nice touch to represent Wren's bisexuality.

Music started playing, and everyone stood up.

The aisle looked like it had been sprayed with glitter

because it was sparkly white. Perfect to represent Tom's wonderfully unique personality.

Charlie walked down the aisle first. I winked when he walked past us, and he smiled. Then the music changed, and I saw Tom holding his mom's hand.

"Oh my god, he looks amazing," Alexi gasped.

Tom's eyes never left Wren's as he took his steps toward the man he loved. I identified so much with the feeling since Charlie and I were coming up on our first anniversary. It still felt like yesterday.

It was no surprise Tom's outfit was daring but stylish and something only someone with his sense of fashion could pull off.

He had black slacks and a white shirt, but it was the corset vest he wore that stole the show. It was royal blue with gold plates showing the structure of the corset. It fit absolutely perfectly on him.

Tom's mom looked the picture of motherly pride, and there were two photos of his dads next to Charlie. They, too, were part of today's celebration.

The ceremony itself was short but beautiful. The only time I took my eyes off the grooms was to look at my husband, who was trying so hard not to cry.

When Tom and Wren were pronounced husband and husband, everyone cheered, and as they kissed, there was a shower of rainbow confetti dropped on the grooms and guests.

The temperature wasn't as cold today as it had been in the past few days, but even so, I was glad to go inside the reception room.

I looked for the grooms' table where Alexi and I would sit next to Charlie.

Slade waived, already waiting for Aiden at the other end of the table.

There was more music as the emcee announced, "Beautiful guests of this celebration, please raise your glasses to welcome the grooms, Mr. and Mr. Jones-Mason."

Wren and Tom walked in hand-in-hand, their smiles showing us all the love they had for each other.

"Hey," Charlie said, sliding next to me. "I tried, I really did, but it was too emotional."

"I know, baby. It's your best friend's wedding. You can cry."

Tom and Wren took their places but stayed up.

There was a microphone on the table, which Wren tapped to check it was on.

"Hello, everyone. Thank you for being here today to witness and celebrate our marriage. I think you'll all agree I'm the lucky one for having this kind, smart, stunning man in my life." He turned to Tom. "Angel, I've given you my vows more than once—"

"Is that what they're calling it these days?" Troy, Wren's brother, shouted, and Wren gave him the finger. Everyone laughed.

Wren continued, "I could write many more, but there's only one thing that matters, and that is that my love for you will only grow as we get older. I wish your dads were here so I could thank them for bringing you into the world, but I know I'll get to meet them one day in a long distant future. Until then, I will keep proving myself worthy of you so that when we all meet in heaven, they won't kick my ass."

"You fucking fucker," I heard Tom mutter between his teeth as he buried his face into Wren's chest.

He took a deep breath and then addressed the guests.

"I never thought I was lucky. After all, I lost both my dads before I could keep any memories of them. My mom tells me I'm nothing like them, and that's a good thing. I'll take her word for it." Everyone laughed. It was well known that Tom's mom joked that Tom was more hers than her brother and brother-in-law's because they had been the most boring couple under thirty in Boston.

"But then," Tom continued, "then I met Charlie, and for the first time in my life, I found a soul mate. Someone who loved me even though I drove him insane. And then he gave me the best gift of all, his family. So now I consider myself the luckiest person on earth-apart from Wren, who got to marry me, of course. I'm lucky to have so much goodness and generosity all around me every day. So thank you all for being here. I hope you will dance. Drink all the sparkly drinks, shake your booty like no one's watching, and most of all, don't leave here today before telling someone how beautiful they look."

There wasn't a dry eye in the room, including mine, because Tom's words resonated with everyone. I put one arm around Charlie and another around Alexi and pulled them closer. "I love you both so much. You look beautiful."

"Thanks, Papa, love you too," Alexi replied.

I met Charlie's eyes, and they said what words couldn't.

After the meal, people started moving around the room, catching up with each other, and going to the dance floor after Tom and Wren's first dance.

"Hey, Dad, who's that?" Alexi asked.

"That's Troy. He's Wren's younger brother," Charlie said.

"He's cute."

"And a little too old for you," I added.

He shrugged in that way only teenagers can. "So what if I like older men?"

Charlie laughed.

"I'm going to ask him to dance."

I tried to stop him as he stood up, but Charlie put his hand on mine.

"Baby, let him go."

"But—"

"This is a big step for Alexi. He's comfortable enough with us to talk about a boy he finds cute. Whatever happens, he knows we have his back."

I pulled my husband closer and wrapped my arms around him, kissing his forehead.

I looked around the room at all the happy faces. The couples that had gotten together, some already married, and some getting there soon enough. There were new children and children on the way. Families and found families.

Never had I ever been happier for the press scandal that took me to Chester Falls. Or the happy coincidence that made James my college roommate. Or any of the small but significant life events that led us all to be here today.

Every single one with their own happy ever after.

EPILOGUE

THE MORNING AFTER THE WEDDING

BEN

"Baby," Tristan whispered, caressing my face.

I opened my eyes to meet his. "Morning."

He smiled back. "Want to go for a walk before breakfast?"

I pulled him closer and inhaled into his neck. Tristan had such a unique scent. The mix of his shower soap, his cologne, and his own natural scent was the best thing in the world.

"I have a better idea," I moaned into his skin, pressing my morning wood onto his leg.

He chuckled. "I'd love to take you up on your offer, but how about we wait until we get home later and then we can spend the next two days in bed?"

"Promise?"

"Promise," he said. "Come on, let's get up."

I groaned, but followed him into the shower. Despite going to bed later after the party, I felt rested. There was definitely a benefit to staying at Lexington-Bennett Hall overnight so we could join the grooms and our friends for brunch.

Tom and Wren were leaving for their honeymoon tomorrow and everyone else would be busy with work and Christmas, so it was the last chance for all of us to be together until the next special occasion.

After the shower we walked down to the kitchen.

"Morning Mary," I said to James's housekeeper and general fairy godmother. Mary was such a warm person and had taken care of us like a mother hen when we'd gotten married here last year.

"Morning me darlings," she said in that lovely Irish accent that never failed to put a smile on my face. "You're up early. I suppose you'll need to get used to it with a little one on the way."

"Nine o'clock isn't exactly the crack of dawn, but I don't think you'll see anyone else up much before eleven today," I said.

She winked. "You'd be surprised. Some of yous have just gone to bed."

I looked at Tristan and then back at Mary. "Who?"

"Mary doesn't tell tales." She tapped her nose.

She gave us two carry mugs of coffee, and we walked out to the garden through the kitchen door, leaving Mary with her brunch preparation.

The bitter cold outside made me want to go back inside. Tristan put his arm around me and we walked toward the pond.

"Babe, we might need to keep this short because my nuts will fall off with this cold," I said.

Tristan laughed. "I am quite attached to your nuts, so message received. I just wanted to breathe some fresh air. Remember the day after our wedding?"

"It was a lot less cold then."

"It was, and that day, just like every day before and every day since, I woke up feeling like the luckiest man in the world. To think things could have been so different had I not caught my ex cheating on me."

I held Tristan closer. We'd both had our share of heartache before we'd found each other, but life was pretty perfect now, and it was about to become even better.

"I still can't believe we're going to be parents," I said.

"I can't wait. How long do you think we need to wait until we know if we're having a boy or a girl?"

I laughed. "Are you already decorating the room in your head?"

Tristan shrugged. "It's what I do, baby. Our child is going to have the best nursery a baby has ever had."

"They'll have two loving parents and a bunch of uncles and aunts. They're already the luckiest kid," I said.

Tristan stared at me. The hand not holding the coffee cup coming up to my cheek. "I have some news for you."

"Oh yeah?"

"Do you remember when I submitted a bid to work on that new hotel in Martha's Vineyard?" he asked.

I did. Tristan had worked day and night around his job for the opportunity to decorate the bedrooms of a new LGBT-inclusive hotel. The owners already owned a large chain of hotels and resorts, and Tristan wanted the opportunity to get his name as an interior designer out there.

"I remember. All those nights we stayed awake. Me writing and you drawing and picking fabrics and patterns," I said.

He smiled. "I had an email from them this morning. They want me to work with them."

I gasped. "Oh my god, Tristan. That's amazing! You totally deserve it. You worked so hard."

He sighed. "There's only one problem. I'll need to be away for three months."

"We can work it out. Maybe I'll even go there for a weekend so you can show me around." The thought of a short break away sounded great.

"It means I might miss some of the baby appointments."

I put my hand over his on my cheek. "Yes, it'll suck a little, but this is your career. You've been there for me as I published my first book, and as I handed over to Ellie more of the running of Bookmark so I could focus on writing. It's your turn now, and I'll be right there with you."

"I'll definitely be back before the baby is due. I wouldn't miss that for the world, you hear me?"

"I know." I pulled him down for a kiss that warmed me from the inside out. Just what I needed. "What do you say we go back inside and start making up for the time you'll be away?"

Tristan smiled against my lips. "I knew I married a smart man."

KRIS

I wrapped my arms around Charlie from behind as he stood by the window, gazing out at the gardens.

"Which one of us is going to pretend we didn't hear Alexi going to his room just now?" I asked, kissing the back of his neck.

"Not me, I'm the cool dad," he said.

I blew a raspberry on his skin and tightened my hold on him as he laughed and tried to get away. "Are you saying I can't be the fun dad?"

"Oh, you are plenty fun." He turned and draped his arms over my shoulders. "But I still think you should be the one to talk to Alexi about boundaries and safety. I'll tackle the other issue."

"So, you don't mind talking to him about being up all night with another boy, but you don't want to talk about him not telling us he was going to be out, or making sure he had security with him?"

Charlie smiled, which made me want to kiss him until his skin was flushed and he was begging to jump back into bed.

"Baby, he was with Troy, who's the most responsible teenager I've ever met. I like that they've become friends, and now even Alexi has a reason to come back to Chester Falls to visit."

I smiled. "Oh, my sweet Charlie, never change."

"What do you mean?" he asked, with a less than impressed expression.

"Two words, baby. Teenage boys."

He opened his mouth and closed it again.

"No. He's too young, I'll—"

I had to tighten my hold on Charlie before he tried to snake his way out of my arms and into Alexi's bedroom.

"Like you said, Troy is a responsible teenager and so is Alexi."

"But—"

I kissed him then until he writhed against me. Our erections rubbing against each other under our pjs.

"Tell you what," I said against his lips. "Let's let this one slide. Alexi couldn't be in a safer place and he's surrounded by people who already love him dearly. How about we go back to bed and make out like teenagers?"

"I could get on board with that."

I picked Charlie up until he had his legs wrapped around my waist, and carried him back to bed. We'd be a little late, but I was sure we could still play the jetlag card.

An hour later, we were dressed and ready to join the group for brunch.

"You look like you've been ravished within an inch of your life, my love," I said into Charlie's ear as we approached Alexi's room.

"Thanks. That's what I was going for." He rolled his eyes.

I smiled without an ounce of regret. Lazy mornings were rare for us, so I'd made the most of the opportunity.

Charlie knocked on Alexi's door. It took a couple of tries until a very sleepy Alexi emerged.

"Good morning, kiddo. You don't seem ready for brunch," Charlie said. I had to give him credit for not sounding as if he knew exactly what Alexi had been up to.

"Um...I'm not hungry. Can I go back to sleep?" he asked, scratching his head and messing his hair even more.

"Are you feeling okay, sweetheart?" I asked. "Do we need to call a doctor?"

Alexi's eyes bulged. "No! No...um...I..." His eyes went first to Charlie and then at me. "I was up with Troy."

"Okay..." Charlie said.

"We didn't do anything. I swear. We just played some games on his laptop and he showed me some cool stuff he's working on for his college application. That's all."

I tried not to meet Charlie's eyes because I wouldn't hold it together, and I wasn't sure Alexi would appreciate his fathers' amusement at his expense.

Charlie took a step toward the door and pulled Alexi into a hug. "Thank you for telling us. Troy is great and I'm glad you found a friend here."

"Just so you know, if you do more than...um...become more than friends, we're okay with it," I said.

Alexi's face went so pink it reminded me of Charlie.

"Can I go back to sleep?" he asked shyly.

"Sure. We'll ask Mary to keep some food aside for you."

He nodded. "Um...Dad and Papa, could we stay in Chester Falls a few days longer?"

Charlie smiled at me.

"I'm sure we can," I said. "Any particular reason?"

"Grandad said I could help him with the New Year's barbecue. He said I'm old enough to learn how to grill a good steak. And Troy said there's a New Year's party at his place. Can we go?"

I was going to reply, but Charlie squeezed my hand.

"Let's talk about the party later, okay?" he said. "As for

grilling steak with your granddad...let's ask Uncle John about that."

"Because he's a firefighter?" Alexi asked.

Charlie laughed. "Something like that."

We left Alexi to catch up on his sleep and went down to the dining room. Ben and Tristan were already there, sitting on one of the couches by the fireplace.

"Wow, Mary really went all out today," I said. "I wonder if I can convince James to lend her to me."

Tristan laughed. "I don't think it's James you need to convince. Connor would have a harder time letting go.

Despite the spread on the table, we sat on the opposite couch, drinking coffee and waiting for the other guys. I wondered if there was a bet going as to who'd be the last couple down.

WREN

"Oh fuck...right fucking there...holy mother..."

The longer I kept up the pace the more Tom cursed. Thank goodness the wedding suite was one floor up from the other rooms.

"Jesus, Angel. You feel so good...so tight."

With every pass of my cock over Tom's prostate I felt as if I was being sucked into his body. I would never tire of this. Of being so far inside my husband I couldn't tell us apart.

My husband.

The thought that I got to call Tom mine for the rest of

our lives was so powerful and all-consuming it triggered my orgasm. It seemed to have gone on forever as I filled him until there was nothing left of me.

"Fuck, baby. I'm so sorry," I said, breathing heavily onto his neck.

He chuckled. "If you hadn't given me six ground-shaking orgasms already, I might be upset that I didn't get to come with your magic dick inside me."

"I'll make it up to you with my magic mouth."

I moved down the bed, replacing my cock with my fingers inside Tom.

He moaned as I found his prostate and then let out a loud, "oh fucking yes with sprinkles on top. Keep up with that and I'll come before you put that mouth on me."

"That's not happening, Angel. I want to drink you down to the last drop like a love potion." I lowered my mouth to his cock and sucked the head.

"Wren!"

He bucked his hips up to get more of himself into my mouth, and I let him. I gagged when he touched the back of my throat, and pulled back out a bit before sucking him all the way down again.

Within seconds, Tom was back to his unintelligible words. I could barely guess what he was saying, but it didn't matter because I understood his body down to the last atom.

"Sprinkles, I'm close."

I looked up to meet his eyes, relishing when I saw the raw need in them. Gag reflex be damned, I sucked Tom's cock with everything I had until I felt the first spurt of his hot, salty cum hitting my throat.

He jerked in a full body orgasm, as if he was trying to suck my fingers farther inside his body. My only regret was that it wasn't my dick.

"I think I'm dead, Sprinkles. You killed me deader than dead."

I rose from the bed to grab a washcloth. When I was satisfied that my man was clean and comfortable, I snuggled up to him. Or rather, I let him snuggle up to me.

"Happy first day of being married," he said.

"Ditto, baby."

"Will it always be like this?" he asked.

"Like what?"

He ran his hands over my chest and abs. "Soul-consuming. Earth-shattering. Perfect."

"It will be, Angel. I promise."

He hummed and snuggled closer.

"You know we need to get up and join the guys, right?"

"I know...but five more minutes. My legs feel like wet noodles. Not to mention other parts of my anatomy."

I chuckled. "I hope that teaches you a lesson."

"Yup. Next time we're getting married I won't behave like a virgin maiden and decline all sex for a week before the wedding."

I kissed his forehead. "Baby, I was thinking more along the lines of not committing to see people for at least a week."

Tom raised his head to face me. "Are you really serious? You'd want to marry me again?"

"Baby," I said, meeting his lips with a gentle kiss. "I'd marry you every single day for the rest of my life, so you can bet your sweet ass that we'll be doing this again."

"I love you, Sprinkles."

"Love you too, Angel."

A loud meow was followed by Coco jumping onto the bed to snuggle between us. It was getting harder for her to move around like she used to. Micah had said she was due to have her kittens in three weeks' time.

"Good morning, gorgeous momma," Tom cooed, and Coco replied as usual, loving all the attention. "Wren, are you sure it's safe for us to go on honeymoon with her like this?"

"Micah said it's fine. We'll be back in plenty of time, and she's staying with him so she couldn't be in better hands. The question is...do you want to know where we're going?"

Tom nodded fiercely.

I considered drawing it out, but I'd already been keeping this from him for so long I was dying to get his reaction.

"We're going to Paris for a week so we can visit all the places you talked about."

I expected many reactions from Tom, but tears weren't it.

"Baby..." I held him closer.

"Thank you so much. I don't even have words that can explain how much this is my dream honeymoon."

"I know, baby. That's why we're going."

"Are we really spending Christmas in Paris? It seems so unreal." He sat up. "Oh my god, I'll need to start thinking about my outfits right now."

I grabbed his hand and pulled him back down to my chest. He came happily. "I'm almost scared to tell you where we're staying."

"We could stay under a bridge for all I care. We'll be in Paris!"

I chuckled. "So, I should cancel the Ritz?"

Tom gasped again. "Are you..." he looked up at me. "You're not joking."

I shook my head.

Tom stared at me for a long time.

"You okay, baby?"

"I must be having a dream. That's the only explanation for what's happening."

"Thomas Angel Jones-Mason, if this is a dream, then I never want to wake up, but I can assure you it's all real. You, me and Paris, baby."

Tom's smile lit up the room. "It's going to be epic."

JAMES

"Where are you going?" I asked, but it was a redundant question because I already knew. Connor stared at me as if I was crazy for asking.

"In case you forgot, we have quite a few guests today and the cleanup crew coming in."

I rose from the bed, walking past Donnie and the turtle tank to stop my husband.

"What are you doing? Stop undoing my buttons. I need to get dressed."

"Connor, baby, you need to get naked and in bed right this moment."

He sighed. "I want to but—"

"The guests. Yes, I'm well aware we have guests. Did you know you talk in your sleep when you're stressed? I know exactly how much you have to do today because you told me repeatedly. I'm surprised you're not exhausted."

He stared at me. "More the reason to let me go."

"No."

"No?"

I shook my head. "No."

He crossed his arms. "How are you going to make me stay?"

I smiled and quirked a brow. As if I didn't already know what made my husband tick.

Had I been dressed, I'd have slowly removed my clothes, but that wasn't an option. I ran my hands over Connor's arms, down to his waist and over his crotch. It was lighter than a feather, but I could tell from the change in his breathing he wasn't unaffected.

Connor always loved being touched and teased until he couldn't hold it in any longer and then took charge, which was exactly my intention.

I turned him so he faced the chest of drawers. As if he knew what was coming, he leaned over and placed his hands on the edge.

"James," he gasped as I lowered his underwear down past his butt cheeks.

"Do you still want to get out, baby?"

"I need to," he said, even though his body was telling a different story.

I put a hand on either cheek to open him up and licked

him from his taint all the way up his crease. He tasted divine and familiar. My own flavor of man.

"Ngh," he moaned. I kept going until I was convinced the only thing in his mind was getting off. "Please, baby..."

"I know what you need, Connor. I'll make it good."

"You always do."

"Wrap your hand around your cock."

He obeyed, cursing as I sought entry with my tongue, not stopping until he was close enough. Giving him pleasure always got me going, so I was hard as a rock and begging to be touched.

Connor groaned when I stopped, but I stood and turned him to face me. When he saw my cock, he pulled me closer, taking us both in his hand.

I pushed him against the chest of drawers. It was likely uncomfortable on his back, but he didn't seem to mind.

"I'm so close, baby," I said before I slammed our mouths together.

We both came shortly after.

"You're the devil," he complained, although he didn't seem too upset that I'd derailed his plans.

"Maybe I am."

"We need a shower."

"Now you're talking." I took him by his hand to our bathroom, where we washed each other while we made out.

"Why were you so adamant about me not going to work?" he asked as we were getting dressed.

"Baby, you've been working like a madman for weeks. You need a break. And you need to rely more on the staff. There's literally a dozen staff around that can guide the cleaning crew. Mary has brunch under control. There's nothing to worry about today other than being with your friends."

He sighed. "I know, you're right. I just really wanted this wedding to be perfect for Tom and Wren."

"It really was, sweetheart. Come on, let's join the guys. Who do you think hasn't made it out yet?" I asked.

Connor glanced at the clock on the bedside table. It was ten-thirty. "All of them?"

I was surprised to find Ben, Tristan, Charlie, Kris, Tom and Wren already in the dining room. They were all chatting in front of the fire.

"Wow, I'm impressed," I said, and everyone laughed.

"We're taking bets," Tristan said.

"Now *that* doesn't surprise me at all. My money is on Aiden and Slade. Aiden is leaving tomorrow for a short book tour and won't be back until Christmas day. We'll be lucky if Slade lets him out of the room at all."

TATE

The guys were in intense discussion as we walked into the dining room.

"Dammit," Wren said. "I'm out already."

"What's going on?" Indy asked.

"We're taking bets as to who's going to be the last ones down."

I said Sergei at the same time Indy said Rory. We high-fived each other, and Ben wrote down our bet.

"How's the baby prep, guys?" Tristan asked.

Indy looked at me, and I couldn't help smiling back and running my hand over his long hair. We'd just had a shower together and he'd left it down. It was a rare because he usually had it up in a bun for work, but to me he was never so relaxed as when he had his hair down, literally.

"We're all set. All we need now is for the little man to arrive," I said.

"Have you picked a name?" Charlie asked.

"We have a few in mind, but we decided to pick when we meet him," I said.

Indy poured coffee into two cups and gave me one, settling against me.

We'd taken some time off a few months ago, and despite renewing our vows in Vegas, the trip had been quite chilled.

Bubble had come through in the last few weeks, too. He was going to do a placement with Tom in a few months, but he was also a talented baker and he'd worked things out with Indy to make sure he could spend as much time with the baby as possible.

Hannah had things covered for us in the practice, so really all we needed was for our little man to decide it was time to meet us.

"Sweetbuns, is that your phone?" I asked when I felt a buzz against my leg.

Indy pulled the phone out and went pale. "What's the matter?"

He looked at me, his eyes wide. "It's time."

"For food? Shouldn't we wait for the others?" We'd been up for a while, so I wasn't surprised my man was starting to feel a little peckish. Usually by now he'd be on his third cup of coffee at least, and about to have lunch since he had such an early start to the day.

"No, Tate. It's time for us to be parents."

"Are you serious?"

He nodded. "We need to get to the hospital."

I stood and took Indy with me.

"Guys..."

Tom got up from Wren's lap and gave us both a hug. "You'll be okay. Send us photos as soon as you can."

"Okay."

The next few hours were a blur.

I couldn't remember how we'd reached the hospital. Only that we did, just in time to get to the delivery room as our beautiful, healthy, baby boy came into the world with the most perfect set of lungs.

One of the most memorable times in my life was the first time I'd kissed Indy—the way his deep blue eyes had shown how much he'd wanted me, how he'd been so ready to give in to the attraction between us.

Now, watching him hold our son for the first time, I had a new moment. Another one in a long list of moments since we'd met, and a precursor to many more to come for the rest of our lives.

Indy turned to me. "He's so perfect."

"He looks just like you, baby. So yes, he is." I placed a kiss on his hair and put my arm over his shoulder as he held the baby against his naked chest.

The world around us faded to nothing as we bonded as a family. My turn to hold our son couldn't come soon enough. The nurses had told us how important this step was for the baby.

I glanced over at our surrogate. She was a picture of exhaustion, but she was beaming as she looked at us.

"Thank you so much for giving us such a precious gift. We'll forever be indebted to you," I said.

She smiled. "Let's call it even."

I nodded. Two years ago, I'd helped her with an extremely difficult divorce from a controlling husband, and custody battle. Her case may have been one of the small triggers that had made me question my job in Boston.

When her name had come up as we searched for a surrogate, I was unsure at first but after meeting with her, Indy and I had agreed she was perfect.

I turned back to my husband and our bundle of cuteness. Seriously, no newborn kid should've been this adorable.

"Do you want to hold him?" Indy asked.

I removed my shirt and held my arms out nervously as Indy placed our son on my chest.

He was so tiny and soft I was afraid I'd break him.

Those little baby sounds he made as he settled against me did me in, and before I knew it, tears ran down my face.

"Hello, little man. I promise I usually have it a little more together, but damn you and your cute little button nose and those big blue eyes," I said.

Indy cleared the tears away.

"How about Tyler?" he said.

I gazed at the baby in my arms and said, "Tyler Isaac Moonshine Brooks."

Indy gasped. "You...you want him to have my grand-mother's surname?"

I nodded and smiled at my husband. "She's a big part of

who you are, and you'll agree that it sounds better than Birch Brooks."

He pressed our lips together and then placed his hand over Tyler's head, gently smoothing his dark mop of hair.

"Thank you," he said.

"Baby, I have so much more to thank you for, it would take a lifetime."

He smiled. "It's a good thing we have a lifetime."

We took a photo of the three of us to send to the guys before Tyler became a little fussy, so the nurse took him away for his full health check.

"I guess we can bring out that *My First Christmas* stocking after all," I said, and Indy rolled his eyes. He'd teased me to no end when I bought it because we were still a whole year away from celebrating our first Christmas with our son.

As it turned out, he was as eager to meet us as we were to meet him.

RYAN

I stomped my boots outside the front door. It hadn't stopped snowing since this morning, and we hadn't had a chance to buy a mat for the foyer of our new place.

When we'd gotten together, I'd moved to Luca's apartment, but then his lease was up just at the time this house had gone up for sale. We knew we were staying in Lydovia for good. We both loved our jobs and had made friends here, so it made sense to set down roots and buy a place together.

It was hard living away from family, especially since all I had was my mom, and now even Santi was in Chester Falls.

We'd just need to make time to go back home more often, which was something I'd been planning on for the new year. I just needed to stop stalling.

"Babe?" I called from the door as I removed my boots and hung my coat. The house was warm, which meant Luca had been home from work a few hours already.

"Bedroom," he answered.

I stopped as I reached the first step of the staircase and saw the glow coming from the living room. The coffee table had candles lit and set with two plates, cutlery, and champagne flutes.

Luca moving in the bedroom caught my attention, so I went up the staircase.

"Are we having a—" My words caught in my mouth when I saw Luca was wearing nothing but a pair of boxer shorts. That itself wasn't unusual. Every time he bought a new pair, he'd parade around virtually naked, to gauge my reaction.

It usually ended up with us falling over each other in bed.

Today's pair didn't have a fun design like the hot dogs ones, or the ones with the bees or the doughnuts. This pair had wedding rings.

I swallowed, my throat dry. My mind running a hundred miles per hour. Also, because Luca was bent over, looking behind the chest of drawers, giving me the best view of his ass.

"Sorry, my um...thing fell behind here," he said, stretching his arm behind the piece of furniture. "Got it."

He stood and turned, placing his hands behind him. "You were saying?"

I couldn't remember what I was about to say because my eyes zeroed in on the small bow tie at the front of his boxer shorts.

Did he know what I'd planned? Surely it was a coincidence. Right?

"I must be losing my touch."

"What?" I asked.

He smiled. "I must be losing my touch if you're still standing by the door, fully dressed, when I'm standing in front of you almost naked."

I closed the distance between us and slammed my mouth onto his. He smelled of pine and citrus from his shower soap, and he smelled of Luca. My friend. My love.

He let me command the kiss, opening up for me as soon as I demanded entry into his hot mouth. I pressed him against the chest of drawers and felt as he became harder.

When he started kissing me back and making his own demands, I let him.

My shirt lost a couple of buttons as Luca rushed to get his hands on me. Our lips parted so we could take an essential breath, but we never stopped touching.

"Jesus, baby. You'll never not make me hot for you. You hear me? You could wear a yeti suit and I'd still want to be the fur up against your skin," I said, sucking on his neck, hoping to leave a mark.

"We need a new rule," He groaned when he struggled with my belt.

"What's that?"

"Get naked at the door."

I chuckled and helped him get me out of my trousers.

Before things went any further I took him by his hand and led him over to the bed.

"Now you're talking," he said. "God, I've been horny for you since this morning when I saw you'd stolen my Christmas tree boxer shorts.

"I think they look good on me. Cleverly positioned decorations and all," I said.

He straddled me and kissed me again, but this time it was slower and more drawn out. The rushed heat turned into slow lovemaking, even before we were fully naked.

"I need you to ask me, Ryan. I can't wait any longer," he said, stopping the kiss and raising his head to gaze into my eyes.

I stared at Luca, seeing in his eyes a vulnerability I hadn't seen in a long time.

When he'd turned sixteen, he'd told his parents he didn't want a birthday party or presents. He'd asked if they could all visit his uncle in Virginia. He had a big ranch with horses and cattle.

Of course, Santi had asked if I could come too, and Luca had said yes. Most of the time we'd spent at the ranch, Luca was always with me. Santi, the daredevil he was, had spent most of the time riding horses and taking part in tractor races with his cousins.

Since Luca and I had gotten together, I started thinking back to some of the memories I had of growing up around the Torres household.

It was clear as day now that Luca had made it his

mission to become closer to me. And I'd been so happy with any little stolen moment pretending to be just a friend that I hadn't even noticed that Santi always left us alone for long periods of time. That most other kids would have wanted their group of friends to join them for birthdays or even just to hang out, but not Luca.

Every time my mind stumbled across an old memory I saw it through a new lens and fell in love with Luca all over again.

"Luca..."

"I know you were going to. Weren't you? I heard Sergei talking with Kris weeks ago. Oh god, you changed your mind." He dropped his head on my chest, shielding his face from me.

I ran my hands over his dark hair. "What exactly did you hear, baby?"

He raised his head slowly. "He said you were going to ask me to marry you this Christmas."

I put my arm around Luca and turned sideways so I ended up half on top of him. "It's not Christmas yet."

He huffed. "I know, but—"

"But if you waited, then you wouldn't be my beautiful, strong, impulsive, grab-the-bull-by-its-horns, Luca. You wouldn't be the man who had the guts to kiss me first and make me face my attraction to you. You wouldn't be the man I've wanted to marry since I was eighteen and saw you wearing a suit to your cousin's wedding and imagined what you'd look like on your wedding day. Luca Torres, will you marry me?"

Luca pulled me down and wrapped his arms around my shoulders.

"Yes. Oh my god, yes. Are you serious? You're not asking just because I made you, right?"

I chuckled and reached over Luca to the bedside table. I opened the drawer and took out the small velvet box I'd been keeping there for months.

Inside were two matching rings I'd picked because the pattern on them were like the woven branches of a tree. The rings spoke to me of our lives growing up together, our relationship strong and solid. Nothing would ever break us apart.

Luca gasped. "You had rings and everything."

"Baby, I've wanted to put a ring on your finger for longer than I care to admit."

He kissed me again. "I love you so much, Ryan."

"I love you too, Luca," I said against his lips. My hands roamed his body until I felt his boxer shorts. "Can I ask you a question?"

"You already did. My answer is yes. Every time you ask, it'll be yes."

I laughed. "I was going to ask about your boxer shorts and the setup in the living room."

He shrugged. "Power of suggestion."

"You thought that wearing underwear with wedding rings and setting up a romantic dinner by the fire would make me propose to you?"

He took the ring box from my hand and put one ring on his finger and the other on mine.

"It seems that it worked," he said with a smug smile.

I shook my head in disbelief. "Don't ever change, baby."

"The only thing I intend on changing is my marital status."

SLADE

I closed my eyes and went under the water spray. Aiden rubbed my back slowly and methodically. His erection poked my thigh, but I knew he didn't want me to do anything about it.

After a round of ground-shaking sex, he just wanted to cuddle and shower.

When we'd first gotten together, I tried to keep up with his, much quicker, refractory period. I didn't believe that he could want to just be with me, touch me, and let me touch him without taking things further. After all, I still remembered being his age and any excuse to get off was an opportunity I didn't miss.

But I soon accepted my limitations and now I really enjoyed this slow after-sex time.

"I really don't want to leave," he said.

I turned in the shower to face him. "It's only a few days."

He sulked. "But I'm going to miss all the Christmas prep."

"Babe, *you* did all the Christmas prep. I have a list of things to do longer than my business plan." I grabbed the shampoo bottle and squirted a dollop onto my hand, then I rubbed my hands together and ran them over Aiden's hair.

"This is our first Christmas together. I want it to be perfect, and now we have Davey, I feel like I'm leaving everything for you to do," he said.

Davey, or Davidson, was the kitten Harley had decided to adopt when we'd gone to Vegas. Aiden claimed Harley had named herself so it was his turn to name the kitten, and apparently, we couldn't have a Harley without a Davidson.

You know you're really in love with your man when you not only accept such ridiculousness in your life; you welcome it.

"It will be the best Christmas, because we'll be together. And don't worry about Davey. Harley takes care of him and I've never seen him stray away from her." I knew I sounded sappy, but I still couldn't believe I'd been lucky enough to have a man like Aiden fall for me.

I'd spent so many years with Mike, but Aiden knew me better. That had been my fault, but I couldn't go back in time and change things. Knowing I'd end up with Aiden, I wouldn't have changed a single second of my life anyway.

Whatever anyone thought, I didn't care. For Aiden I'd be a hopeless romantic, a romance novel-worthy boyfriend, and anything else he wanted.

"Are we still going to my parents' for New Years?" he asked. "We don't have to, you know."

"I know. But they're raising money for a cause that is very close to me. If us showing up and smiling for some pictures helps them, then I'll wear that penguin suit, whatever it takes.

I'd met Aiden's parents and we'd gotten to know each other a little better. I had a feeling that for the first time, they were also getting to know their son better.

They threw a New Year's party every year to raise money for charity, and this year they were supporting a charity that helped older kids in foster care. The ones no one really wanted. The ones like me.

Now I knew there was no chance of my past catching up with me, I wasn't as shy about being on camera. In fact, Aiden had shared some photos of us on his social media, and his fans had gone wild.

There were all kinds of rumors about what he'd been doing in his year off, and if he'd just been spending time with his new sexy, silver fox boyfriend.

I wasn't so sure about the sexy, silver fox label, but if it helped Aiden's business and made his fans happy, then I was happy, too.

"Shall we get dressed and go down for brunch?" he asked.

"Yeah, let's do it. I could murder some coffee right now."

"Babe. Same."

There was animated chattering coming from the dining room. As soon as we walked in, there were a few cheers.

"Sup guys," I said.

"Damn you," Connor said. "Couldn't you have stayed in bed making out, or something?"

I laughed and saw Aiden's ears go a little pink.

"Let me guess, you have a bet going."

SANTI

"We should probably get up and go down to brunch," Micah said, not moving an inch from where he was plastered to my body.

He drew patterns with his fingers on my chest. I wasn't sure he was spelling something or was just mindlessly moving them around.

"It's still nighttime," I said, unable to keep the smile from my face.

"That trick worked for maybe three seconds, once. Open your eyes and you'll see the light."

"I have," I said, opening my eyes, but instead of gazing out of the window at the large estate, I focused on the most beautiful thing I'd ever see—Micah's face.

This close, I could see it so well. His thick beard, his warm eyes, that little spot hidden under the beard that only I knew about, and my favorite, his lips.

He smiled and brought his hand up to touch my face. His eyes were closed as he traced all the different lines and dips that made me.

I spent my time memorizing him. Getting ready for the day when I could no longer simply open my eyes and see him. I used to be afraid of it, but that feeling was receding because I was also learning what he looked like with the tips of my fingers.

I used the way he smelled, and I trained my ear to know when he was smiling even without a sound.

For months now, Micah had been doing the same. Not because he needed to, but because he wanted to know how it felt. He wanted to be able to explain what he saw in a way I would understand.

The day he'd told me the reason why he touched me so

much with his eyes closed, I'd lost my heart to him all over again.

Who knew? Santi Torres, the daredevil playboy, finding his happiness in all the simple things. I couldn't have done it without Micah. That was for sure.

"I feel like we should be having all the pet-free, noisy sex we can get away with right now," he said.

I chuckled. "I thought we'd already accomplished that last night."

He hit my chest playfully. "You know what I mean."

"Linda is happy to keep an eye on the kids, so what do you say if we ask Connor and James if we can stay another night? Maybe tomorrow we could talk to them about having our wedding here."

Micah opened his eyes and raised his head. "Are you serious?"

"I am."

He slammed his mouth against mine and kissed me until I was considering the lazy morning in bed as a serious option.

"Come on, let's go to brunch so we can come back here and have all the sex," he said. "You know I'm still making up for lost time."

I laughed. "Baby, if we make up any more for lost time, both our dicks will fall off."

"They won't. I'm a doctor, I know these things," he said matter-of-factly before getting off the bed.

By the time we got down to the dining room, everyone was sitting by the fireplace, either on the various couches or on the carpet.

"Yes!" Indy and Tate both shouted, high-fiving each other as we came in.

"What's going on?" Micah asked.

"We had a bet going about who was going to be the last couple down. We voted for Rory and Sergei," Indy said. "Since you're both here now and they're not, we win."

"Did anyone vote for us?" Micah asked.

There was a pause. I couldn't see who was keeping track of the voting but then Ben said, "No, no one voted for you."

I pulled Micah closer and placed a kiss on his head. "Then you should have because you'd have won."

"But Rory and Sergei aren't here," Charlie said.

"That's because they went home last night."

RORY

I wasn't sure what I noticed first when I woke up. That Sergei wasn't in bed with me, or the smell of burnt toast.

The sound of a few swear words brought a smile to my face. Exactly how much toast had Sergei burnt if I could smell it all the way in the bedroom?

I got up to use the bathroom and then put my pajama pants on before I went downstairs to the kitchen.

Sergei was wearing nothing but his boxer shorts, so I leaned against the frame of the kitchen door and took my time appreciating the curve of his ass, the muscles on his back rippling with every move he made, the thick thighs that felt amazing when they were wrapped around me.

I was also ignoring the hurricane that seemed to have gone through the kitchen. There were pots and pans every-where, a broken bowl on the table, flour where flour shouldn't be, and I was pretty sure the coffee machine was plotting its escape from the hell that had descended upon it.

"Good morning," I said.

Sergei turned around, looking more than a little flustered. "You're supposed to be in bed."

"My house doesn't normally smell like someone's trying to set fire to it very slowly, so call it self-preservation, but I had to check what it was. Besides," I said, walking up to him. "You weren't there."

He wrapped his arms around me and kissed me. A good morning kiss that would have led to other things if we'd still been in bed.

"I know what you're thinking," he said.

"Oh, really?"

He placed his hands on my ass, pressing us closer together. His dick was hard, and I bit my lip, wondering if it would be too forward to drop to my knees right now.

"Yeah. I can tell by the way your eyes have gone darker. The little flush of pink on your neck. But mostly it's the way you're hard for me."

I smiled and tilted my head, which he took as a sign that he should suck on my skin. No complaints from me there.

"Then why did I wake up on my own? And why does it seem like I've been burgled by someone really hungry, but with poor cooking skills?"

He huffed. "I was going to bring you breakfast in bed but I had a few issues."

"You don't say."

He slapped my ass. "I should have you over my knee for being sassy."

"I thought you liked my sass."

"Oh kitten, I more than like your sass." He kissed me again, this time claiming me as his, even though that ship had sailed a while ago. I was already totally his. Except...

"Sergei," I said, almost out of breath from the kiss. "I have to ask you something."

"My answer is yes." He kept trailing kisses down my neck and then picked me up, walking up the stairs to the bedroom with me wrapped around him like a monkey. "You're not hungry for breakfast, are you? Because I need you now, and you don't have bread and I have no idea how your coffee machine works."

He dropped me onto the bed, covering my body with his. My brain stopped working for a moment. "Wait. I can't think when you're doing that."

"Doing what?" He asked with what I now knew was his *oh not so innocent* face.

"Devouring me."

He chuckled. "Okay, ask your question."

"Um, I'm not sure it's a question per se..."

He quirked a brow.

I let out a breath. "I don't know what happens next."

He pressed me farther into the mattress. I groaned at the exquisite feeling of our cocks rubbing together and wondered about the merits of having this conversation naked.

"I know what happens next, and no, I'm not hungry for breakfast. It's just...I don't know what happens next, *next*."

"Kitten, you're going to have to spell it out for me."

"When are you going back to Lydovia? Because it feels like you just got here and I don't know if I'll like not having you around very much, but your life is there so you'll go back and then you'll get busy, and when will you come back to visit. Will you come back to visit? I mean, we're a thing, aren't we?" I was almost out of breath by the time I word-vomited the thoughts that had been plaguing me for the last few days.

"Hey, hey, calm down, kitten. How long have you been worrying about this?"

"Since...you came back and told me you're in love with me? Well, I guess maybe not when we were...you know... those times my brain was pretty occupied, but the rest of the time, yes."

Sergei ran his hand over my hair, letting it rest on my cheek. He didn't laugh at me, or smile. His expression was so serious it made me scared of what he'd say next.

"Baby, I don't think I can stand living apart from you. I've already been on my own for too long. If we're talking about the future, then whether you move to Lydovia, or I move here, it doesn't matter, as long as we're together. If you're talking about the most immediate future, then I'd like to take you back with me to spend Christmas in Lydovia. My mom would love to meet you properly and it's a chance for you to get a feel for the country. Maybe after New Year we can talk about it again. We don't have to make any decisions right now. The only decision that we have to make is if we want to be together."

I let out a relieved sigh. "Yes, that's definitely a yes from me. I want to be with you wherever that may be."

He looked as relieved as I felt.

"Would you really want me to move to Lydovia to be closer to you?" I asked.

He smiled. "Baby, I'd love that very much. For one, it

would give my mom someone else to spoil, but you do what is right for you."

"And what if what's right for me is living with you, in Lydovia, near your mom?"

"Are you sure?"

I shrugged. I wasn't sure of anything other than I'd move to the ends of the earth to be with the only person in my life who made me feel as though I was worthy, important, special. The person who made my heart skip a beat when he walked into the room, and caused the butterflies in my belly to fly whenever he smiled at me with his perfect mouth and beautiful blue eyes.

"I'm sure I want to be with you, and I'd be honored to spend Christmas with you and your mom. As you say, we can talk about it in the New Year and then decide."

Something in my gut told me it would be the best decision I'd ever make.

"By the way, it seems we're personae non grata with the guys," he said.

"Oh shit. I hope Tom's not upset," I said.

After the party last night, we'd gone up to our allocated room at Lexington-Bennett Hall, but I'd suggested we come to my place instead. It meant we had to drive back to Chester Falls quite late, but selfishly, I wanted to wake up to Sergei and not have to rush to a brunch.

In the last couple of days, I'd become more anxious about Sergei's impending departure, so I wanted to hang on to every possible second of each day I could spend alone with him.

"Nah, he's good. Apparently, they had some kind of bet going about something, but I couldn't understand in the voice message. There was too much noise in the background."

"I've heard of their bets. I have a feeling it was wise to leave when we did," I said.

"Anyway..." he said, running his nose over mine.

"Anyway..."

"How about we get naked, get dirty, clean up, and then go out for lunch?"

I kissed his perfect lips. "That sounds like a plan."

As Sergei explored my body inch by inch, I felt I was finally settling into myself. It was as if my soul had spent all my life hovering over my body and it was ready to occupy it.

Every lick, every kiss, brought me down to earth, to a reality I had only dreamed of.

It seemed that after seeing everyone I knew find their match, it was my turn to catch my own happy ever after.

Dear reader,

I hope you enjoyed How to Catch a Happy Ever After.

Writing this book was a little bit of an emotional journey because it's the end of the series and I really struggled to say goodbye to my characters.

I mean, did you see how long that epilogue was? Yeah, I wasn't ready. Not to mention there's still an additional bonus scene if you keep reading.

If you've come along with me on this Chester Falls journey you may have also fallen in love with a few side characters. Maybe you wished they had their own story?

My new is titled Dads of Stillwater, and guess what. It

has all the single dads you can handle plus some of your favorite tropes. And those secondary characters from Chester Falls? You might see two or three find their happy ever after.

After all, Stillwater is only a few miles from Chester Falls.

If you enjoyed How to Catch a Happy Ever After please take a moment to write a review. As an indie author all reviews are important because they help inform new readers.

Be sure to follow me on Bookbub to be notified of new releases, and look for me on Facebook for sneak peaks of upcoming stories.

If you would like to be the first to know when my new releases are available, read exclusive FREE stories and know what I'm up to, please sign up for my newsletter, Ana's VIP Readers: bit.ly/AnaAshley.

For giveaways, sneak peaks, ARC opportunities and general caffeinated fun times, please join my facebook group! Café RoMMance - Ana's Reader Group

WHEN SPYING GOES WRONG

CHARLIE

"Kris?" I called from the door to our apartment in the palace.

Well, Kris's definition of an apartment, that was.

I fondly remembered the two-bedroom place I'd shared with Tom in Boston. Aside from the bedrooms, our living area had basically been the kitchen and a small space—we called it the lounge—only big enough for a couch and a TV. But it was *our* space, and we loved it.

None of the riches. We'd had each other, and it was all we needed.

Of course, finding out the love of your life was a prince hadn't been all bad, per se. Apart from waking up to the most amazing man in the world every day, I also got to do what I'd always dreamed of doing: drawing.

As Kris had promised, I drew when I wanted and because I wanted. Most of my work was donated to charities who auctioned it to raise money to fund their projects, and that's how we ended up becoming a family of three when we adopted our son, Alexi.

Alexi turned eighteen two weeks ago, and he was why I was currently looking for my dear husband in all corners of the palace.

When I didn't find him in our enormous apartment, I walked out, stopping by the music room, one of his favorite places.

"Hello, Charlie. I'll bet my crown you're looking for my brother," Aleks, the Queen of Lydovia and my beautiful, sweet, amazing sister-in-law, said.

She was holding her baby daughter, Arabella. I couldn't resist holding out my arms to snuggle her. Arabella was one of those babies you saw in magazines and couldn't believe were real because they were so beautiful.

Instead of her mother's brown eyes, the same as Kris's, Arabella inherited her father's blue, which, combined with her copper-colored curly hair, made her look like an angel.

Aleks placed Arabella in my arms. Her baby smell filled my senses, making me broodier than I cared to admit.

I cooed at her and replied in a baby voice, "Yes, Mommy is right because Mommy knows her brother very well. And since she will be right, we know Uncle Kris will be in big trouble." I tickled Arabella's tummy, and she giggled.

"Sigh. I really need to stay away from you. You're making me want one of these, and I already have to raise a teenager and an unruly adult." I gave Arabella back to Aleks.

She laughed. "I don't know. Maybe a baby is just what Kris needs to keep him busy." She winked and kissed me on the cheek before walking toward her private apartment.

I thought about what she said.

Could we do it? Could we have a baby now?

We're both so busy, but Alexi will go to college soon. Besides, Aleks is doing it *and* running a country.

Focus, Charlie.

Since I'd already checked all the places within the palace, including his office, which was suspiciously empty, I walked out to the gardens.

"Ah-ha!" Why hadn't it occurred to me to check the royal guards' offices? He often dropped by to check on his friends or for a workout. Although today, I doubted that would be the reason. If that was indeed where he was.

As soon as I entered the main office, Zeke stood up.

"You Royal Highness...um...sorry...Charlie...hi?"

I laughed. I should have caught that moment on camera because you never saw Zeke flustered. Which meant I was close.

He'd also defaulted to my official title, which was something I insisted the guys, especially those closer to Kris, drop. To them, I was just Charlie. It made me feel more normal. There wasn't a day I wasn't proud to be Prince Charles of Lydovia, but sometimes it was nice being just Charlie Williams.

Zeke never had a problem calling me Charlie. Ever.

This meant I was *really* close.

"Would you like a doughnut?" he asked, pointing at the table where several open boxes containing Lydovia's specialty pastry were already half-empty. "Luca brought them in fresh this morning."

"No, thank you," I said. "I take it Sergei and Ryan are

in their office." I pointed to the office at the back of the room.

Zeke looked as though he wasn't sure how to answer the question. I walked over to the office and opened the door. Both desks were empty. Computers off. CCTV monitors on, as usual.

The monitors showed the same footage as those in the main office. I looked at each of the cameras, which were placed mostly in places where it wasn't practical to put an actual guard.

Something caught my attention, so I looked closer.

"Is that...Zeke...is that Ryan walking across the lawn with a large box of popcorn?"

I heard Zeke's resigned sigh. "Yes."

"Where is he going?"

"Oh, Charlie, I was afraid you'd ask me that because I'm bound by law to tell you the truth, but I'll also get my ass kicked by my boss for telling you."

I'd lived at the palace for three years, and I thought I knew it pretty well. Clearly, there were still some places I wasn't privy to.

"If you tell me, I'll make sure that two-week vacation you have coming up gets extended to a month. I know you're planning on proposing to your boyfriend, so I'm sure you'll want more time together. And I'll upgrade your accommodation at the resort you're staying at."

Zeke smiled but looked at Sergei's desk.

"And I'll deal with your boss too."

He hugged me tightly before remembering he wasn't supposed to and straightening. I laughed.

"They're at the bunker."

"The bunker?"

"Oh man, they're going to kill me for this," he said.

"*Who* exactly are they?"

"Kris, Sergei, Rory, Ryan, and Luca."

Suddenly, I was a lot more annoyed. "Why was I cut out?"

He looked at me, and I saw nothing but sincerity. "I think you know why. Come with me. And you better give me a good reference if I have to look for another job," he muttered as I followed him out of the office.

We crossed the garden back into the palace, but instead of our usual side, we turned toward the king's quarters.

We never went into the king's quarters unless there was an invitation. Or you were Aleks, of course. Or Mimi. Sergei's mom could run this country if Aleks so desired.

The difference between this part of the palace and ours was considerable. I wondered for a moment if I'd stepped into a medieval castle.

Zeke took me toward a darkened hallway I'd have missed if he hadn't pulled me into it.

I gasped when he stopped halfway and pulled a candelabra from the wall. Suddenly, the wall gave way. Zeke pushed it open, leading to another small hallway. This one was better lit.

"I hope this isn't where you're bringing me to die. I'm too young," I said.

Zeke snorted.

I heard voices that grew louder as we approached the end of the hallway.

Zeke put his hand to his lips so I wouldn't make a sound.

After four years with Kris, I knew him better than he knew himself. And I knew he would do this. I just hadn't known how.

"Seriously? *That* is how he's holding hands? This kid is no good. Add him to the list," Sergei said.

"I have issues with his shoes," Rory said, taking a handful of popcorn as Sergei pulled his chair closer and kissed his head.

"What do you mean?" Kris asked.

"If he can't get his shoes right, what else will he get wrong?" Rory said. "The kid is going out with a prince, and he made no effort. Did he even brush his hair?"

I rolled my eyes. That was coming from the guy who stole my first kiss in my parents' kitchen on Christmas Day, surrounded by leftover food.

"I think they look really cute together. Who knows, maybe they'll be each other's true love," Luca said, leaning into Ryan, who put his arm around his fiancé.

I looked at Zeke, who was smiling and shaking his head.

The large screen in front of the guys played the footage from the royal guard who was supposedly following my son on his first official date.

Alexi knew he'd have security with him, and so did his date. That was standard protocol. But security was told to give them space. After all, Lydovia is a safe country, and I wanted Alexi to have as much of a normal upbringing as possible, considering that, like me, he wasn't born a royal.

The five men in front of me kept a running commentary of my kid's first date as the two boys walked down the street, where there was a movie theater and a few other entertainment venues.

There was a collective gasp as the two boys went inside an Arcade instead of the movie theater, which was clearly what they'd expected from a first date.

"I'm aborting this mission," Ryan said, holding his hand up to his mouth to communicate with the security guard.

I coughed, and all five men turned around at once.

It was quite amusing to see Kris in the middle, looking like he'd been caught with his hands down his pants, and the other two couples staring at Kris, not knowing how to react.

"Charlie, my love. What are you doing here?" Kris asked, standing and coming to greet me with a kiss.

I didn't miss the look he gave Zeke, but I grabbed his chin and made him look at me.

"What's going on here?" I asked, playing dumb.

I didn't say a thing, and everyone else seemed to have also lost their words.

"This is an interesting room. Care to tell me more about it?" I asked, going around Kris and leaning against the large desk in front of the monitor they were watching.

Sergei was the first to talk. "The king ordered this room built to monitor us when he realized we tended to run away from the palace. Aleks learned about it when she became Queen, and therefore, we found out about it."

I put my hand to my chin and stared at my husband.

"And you didn't think this would be information I would want to know?"

To give him credit, he looked really sorry. "I was going to tell you, but it was that time when you went back to Chester Falls for your sister's birthday. When you came back, I missed you, so there were other things I wanted to catch up on more, you know...like naked things...and I forgot."

I raised my hand, feeling the tips of my ears getting hot. "That's enough detail."

"Five grown men see nothing wrong with what's going on here?" I asked, gesturing around the room. The only one who seemed a little embarrassed was Luca.

"Baby, we're trying to protect Alexi. We want the best for him," Kris said.

"So spying on his very first date is the best way to keep him safe? You didn't trust your team of royal guards to do it?"

Sergei looked down at his feet. As one of the two heads of security, he should know best, but he was also one of Alexi's godfathers, so he was stuck between his duty and his heart.

"I'm in a room full of gay men who all had a first date at some point. How awkward was it? Did you want someone watching?" I asked.

"My first date was shit," Ryan said. "All I kept thinking about was how I wished the guy was Luca and how much of a pervert I felt for wanting the guy to be Luca, who had just turned eighteen."

Luca turned his head to Ryan. "You didn't date at all until I turned eighteen?"

Ryan shrugged. "Late bloomer. Or maybe always just in love with you."

"Ugh, don't make me puke the doughnuts I had earlier," Zeke said. "They were too nice."

Everyone laughed.

"Okay, truth time, you perverts," I said.

They all looked at each other in confusion.

"I didn't know what you were planning or that you were this sophisticated. I clearly underestimated you, love of my life," I said to Kris, "but you've underestimated me too."

"What do you mean?"

I laughed. "You've all been following two of Alexi's friends. Jordan is with them to ensure they're safe since one of them is pretending to be Alexi."

Sergei straightened. "Where's Alexi?"

"Calm down, tiger," I said.

"Alexi has been with his boyfriend in the theater room here at the palace, where they can have privacy to watch whatever movie they want"—I walked over to Kris and put my hands on his chest. He wrapped his arms around me automatically—"or not. They have enough snacks to last a week. Alexi promised it won't turn into a sleepover, and he'll check in with us when his boyfriend goes home."

One by one, the guys all left, muttering their disappointment.

Kris took my mouth in a hungry kiss, and I let him, savoring him. After all, I hadn't seen him since this morning.

"You played...what do they call it in America? A good, good cop," Kris says.

"Does that mean you're the bad cop?"

"I must be since I was the one sending the spies after my son. I will apologize to him later."

"You will," I said into his mouth, "but now, how about

we make use of this secret room, and you show me how bad a cop you can really be?"

He locked the door behind us—not that anyone would come in here since the few people that knew about this room were already gone, but better safe than sorry—and stalked over to me.

His kiss was hungry, and as I'd already become accustomed to, Kris had no problem picking me up and dropping me so my ass was on the table. He pushed aside anything that might get in the way, and with a simple gesture, one hand on my chest, asked me to lie back.

Oh fuck.

Sex with Kris was always good, but when he was in a giving mood, it was *gooood*. And from the way his dark eyes stared at me, I could tell he was about to really make up for the errors of his ways.

Not that I was mad at him. At all. Alexi and I had planned his non-escape to the finest detail with our bodyguards, Jordan and Sebastian. How Ryan didn't catch on to it, I don't know, but it was fun.

Kris opened my shirt one button at a time, which I was grateful for. It wouldn't be the first time we'd lost ourselves somewhere in the palace, and *I* was the one to do the walk of shame, having to pull a buttonless shirt closed with my hands while Kris looked like he'd just come out of a magazine photoshoot.

By the time he reached my pants, I was desperate for him to touch me.

"What do you need, baby?"

"You, Kris. Always you. Just fucking touch me. Please."

He chuckled. "I'm going to make this one quick just to

get the edge off, but then we're going to our room and locking ourselves in." He lowered the zipper on my pants and palmed my erection.

"Fuck," I cried.

"Later, baby, later. I'm going to take my time with you until we're nothing but two spent bodies who only belong to each other."

"Yes..."

He lowered the elastic of my boxers, and my erection was in Kris's hot mouth before it even sprung out.

I moaned as he took me to the root before sucking my crown like his favorite lollipop.

"You taste like apple and cinnamon," he said.

"That's because you've been eating popcorn. You better have saved some for—fuck," I shouted as he pulled my balls while his mouth bobbed on my cock.

Since he'd discovered I enjoyed that little bit of pleasure-pain, he'd used it every time he wanted to drive me insane. Not that it took much when it came to Kris.

He just needed to walk into the room.

The screen behind me was still playing with images, but there was no sound. The bodyguards were probably still following the kids, but I didn't care.

The glare from the TV. Kris's hands on me. The need to come. It all became too much.

"Kris," I begged.

Quickly, he stood and unzipped his own pants, pulling his underwear down just enough to release his hard cock.

"Wrap your legs around me, baby."

Fuck, for an orgasm, I'd do anything this man ordered me to do until the end of time.

I did as he said and then gasped as he spat on his hand and held our cocks together, stroking them and bringing us to release.

It didn't take me long because I'd already been close. When he pulled me up so I could kiss him, that was it.

The taste of Kris. His firm grip on my cock, his other arm keeping me secure against him. Perfection.

I came in ripples of pleasure that lasted longer than I expected. Kris followed as if he didn't trust himself to come before I did.

Our breaths mingled as we kissed, ignoring the softening cocks between us.

Fortunately for us, there was a box of tissues nearby, so we cleaned up as much as possible and straightened our clothes before Kris turned off the monitor.

"Do you do much spying from here?" I teased.

"A little," he confessed.

"Oh really? Who do you spy on?"

We walked out of the room, through the creepy hallway, and back into the well-lit palace.

"I spy on you. Have you never seen the camera in the corner of your studio?"

"No. There's a camera in my studio?" I wasn't sure if I felt shocked, angry, or horny.

"When you're working, you have this really peaceful expression. It's like you're making the world right...I don't know how to explain it. It's the only time I see you make that face. I love it. Only I get to see it, no one else."

I leaned on him as we walked to our apartment, and he put his arm around my shoulders.

"You're really romantic, you know that?" I asked.

"Shh, don't say it out loud. I have a reputation to uphold," he said.

I laughed.

"Come on, let's have dinner and wait for Alexi."

When we walked in, Alexi was in the lounge playing piano. When he saw us, he stopped and smiled.

I felt Kris still next to me. If Alexi was back so early, did the date go wrong?

"My goodness, your faces. It's like the apocalypse is coming. A teenager with a broken heart isn't the end of the world, you know," Alexi said.

"Oh, my heart," I couldn't help voice.

"I'll kill the little—"

"Gotcha," Alexi said, laughing at both of us.

Kris and I shared a look of relief before we sat on the large couches. Alexi sat between us, crossed his legs, and sighed.

I smiled at Kris over Alexi's head.

"So..." I said.

"It was really nice." Alexi played with the hem of his jeans. "I think he was a little scared at first, but I told him it takes a while to get used to it all. I used to get scared of the bodyguards too."

I bit my lip as I saw Kris rolling his eyes as if encouraging Alexi to get to the good stuff with the power of his mind.

"We watched a movie and sat on the giant bean bags instead of the seats...so um...we were a little closer...so, anyway, we had snacks and the movie was funny. We laughed a lot, and then he kissed me."

Both Kris and I held Alexi in an embrace.

"Thank you for sharing that with us, sweetheart," I said. "Did you like it? Do you think you'll continue to see this boy again?"

"Of yeah, we did a lot of kissing, but I'm not telling you all of it. Considering you came back home after me, I'll say you were probably doing worse in some corner of the palace the housekeepers now need to bleach." He stood up. "I'm going to bed. Got class tomorrow. Love you."

I stared at Kris, lost for words.

"He's not wrong, baby."

"We were sassed by our own kid," I said.

"We picked well."

I leaned over and kissed him. "That we did. I love you so much, Kris."

"I love you too, baby."

LETTER TO MY READERS

It's no lie when we say it takes a village.

Alpha readers, beta readers, editors, proof-readers, cover artists, software providers, arc teams, Patrons, friends, family, fans...the list goes on. Every person that touches each step of publishing a book plays an important part.

The Chester Falls series changed my life, but I wouldn't be here without the support of some really amazing people.

The first shout out is to Anka, whose endless supply of plot bunnies not only nourishes my creativity, it also makes me laugh on a daily basis.

Tanya and Lisa, my beta readers, who have become good friends but are still never afraid to call it out when I get it wrong.

Rhys Everly-Lawless, from the day we met in a pub in London to today, our friendship has grown stronger and stronger. We call on each other's shit and don't always agree but one thing is absolute, we are in this together, pushing each other to do better and succeed.

Pippa Silver, my sister and one of the few people that truly know me. It's been a privilege to see her grow from making a few graphics for my series promo, to start her own business supporting authors and their brands.

Finally, but definitely not last, my own Froglet. Without his support everything I do would be a lot harder. With his support I took a year off work to work on my writing. With his support I said goodbye to the day job to become a full time author- a dream come true.

Life isn't always easy but together we can do anything we set our minds to.

To every single person out there that has ever picked up one of my books, I have the utmost respect and gratitude. Without you I wouldn't be here doing what I do.

Thank you everyone

Ana

CONNECT WITH ANA

Connect with Ana on social media:

Hang out in my FB Group:
facebook.com/groups/CafeRoMMance
Follow me on instagram: *instagram.com/anawritesmm/*
Follow me on Bookbub: *bookbub.com/authors/ana-ashley*
Sign up to my newsletter: *bit.ly/AnaAshley*

For an overview of all of Ana's books and audiobooks, visit her website: *anawritesmm.com/books*

BOOKS BY ANA ASHLEY

Single Dads of Stillwater
A spin off series from Chester Falls that can be read on its own. Each book features one or more single dads in this community of friends, family and found family. In this contemporary MM romance series you'll find heat, emotion and a guaranteed happy ever after.
Newcomer
Antagonist
Breakthrough
Heartstring
Datebook (Coming early 2024)

Finding You Series
A standalone series set across the Atlantic between New York and Portugal. Find your way home with this contemporary MM romance series with friends to lovers, star-crossed lovers and age gap with plenty of heat, feels and always a happy ever after.
Home Again
Together Again
Love Again
And for a special short story, Complete Again, plus bonus scenes, grab the Finding You boxset now.

Room for 3 series
This is a high heat MMM contemporary romance series set in an island resort.
The Resort
The Vacation (Free short story)

Chester Falls Series
From a Prince to a Happy Ever After for all, enjoy this small town MM romance series that's as sweet as they come, with plenty of heat, humor and everything in between.
How to Catch a Bookworm (Prequel short)

How to Catch a Prince
How to Catch a Rival
How to Catch a Bodyguard
How to Catch a Bachelor
How to Catch the Boss (a Christmas novella)
How to Catch a Biker
How to Catch a Vet
How to Catch a Happy Ever After
You can now have all the books in the series and the prequel all in two
boxsets.
Chester Falls Collection Volume I
Chester Falls Collection Volume II

Standalone books
Christmas Bubble: a low angst, standalone, Christmas novel featuring
a petite but larger-than-life cheerleader, an older demisexual football
coach and a winter cabin by the lake with only one bed. With cameos
from Chester Falls and Stillwater.
Midnight Ash: a sweet Cinderella fairytale retelling with a sexy kinky
twist on the side, and a cast who don't quite behave as you'd expect.
Stronghold: a sweet and sexy romance in Sarina Bowen's World of True
North, Vino & Veritas series. This is a standalone story between two
childhood friends who reunite after as decade apart, with some creative
use of maple syrup.

FREE READS
My Fake Billionaire
The Vacation

ABOUT ANA

Ana Ashley was born in Portugal but has lived in the United Kingdom for so long, even her friends sometimes doubt if she really is Portuguese.

After getting hooked on reading gay romance, Ana decided to follow her lifelong dream of becoming an author.

These days you can find her in front of her laptop bringing her stories to life, or in the kitchen perfecting her recipe for the famous Portuguese custard tarts.

Ana Ashley writes sweet and steamy gay romance set in America, often in small towns where everyone knows everyone.

You can follow Ana on the usual social media hangouts.

For access to exclusive teasers, content, and general book and food related goodness you can now join Ana in her Facebook Group, Café RoMMance - Ana's Reader Group

Ana's VIP Readers - bit.ly/AnaAshley

Facebook Page - @anawritesmm

Email - ana@anaashley.com

Instagram - @anawritesmm
Bookbub - bookbub.com/authors/ana-ashley
Goodreads - goodreads.com/ana-ashley